Praise for Bret Lott and *A Dream of Old Leaves*

"Bret Lott writes about men and women, work and marriage, with a clear-eyed sense of the ways in which we betray—and redeem—ourselves."

—James Atlas

"Probing beneath the smooth surface of suburban domesticity, Mr. Lott's spare, emotionally restrained fictions bring to mind a minimalist John Cheever. . . . The best of these domestic tales are very good indeed."

—*The New York Times Book Review*

"*A DREAM OF OLD LEAVES* is a haunting, memorable collection . . . immediately sympathetic, highly resonant, and sometimes quite funny. . . . Lott makes the mundane sing. . . . He forces a reader, through the accumulation of detail, to feel along with his characters, to perceive one's own truth. . . ."

—*San Francisco Chronicle*

"These are subtle, tightly told tales, often marked by humor and compellingly odd characters . . . carefully constructed and satisfying."

—*Washington Times*

"Lott is almost a miniaturist in his ability to evoke powerful emotions from stories that are, at times, merely slivers of human experience. . . . It takes a consummate artist to bring off the kind of effect Lott seems so effortlessly to achieve."

—*Richmond News Leader*

Also by Bret Lott

THE MAN WHO OWNED VERMONT

A STRANGER'S HOUSE

JEWEL

REED'S BEACH

HOW TO GET HOME

FATHERS, SONS, AND BROTHERS

THE HUNT CLUB

BRET LOTT

A Dream of Old Leaves

WASHINGTON SQUARE PRESS
PUBLISHED BY POCKET BOOKS
New York London Toronto Sydney Tokyo Singapore

For
John Hermann and Jay Neugeboren

The author thanks the publishers of the magazines in which the following stories first appeared:
"A Dream of Old Leaves" in *Redbook;* "Crazy" in *Confrontation;* "Things That Could Come" in *The Antioch Review;* "Brothers" in *The Iowa Review;* "What Our Life Is Like" in *The Indiana Review;* "Work" in *The Seattle Review;* "Rum Cake" ("as Friday, After Work") in *New England Review and Bread Loaf Quarterly;* "What About My Lawn?" in *Gambit;* "Burglars" in *The Missouri Review;* "Garage Sale" in *Willow Springs* and "Sleeping Through" in *Michigan Quarterly Review.*

Grateful acknowledgment is made for permission to reprint excerpts from the following copyrighted works:
"Learning Gravity" from *Skating with Hunter Grace* by Thomas Lynch.

A Washington Square Press Publication of
POCKET BOOKS, a division of Simon & Schuster Inc.
1230 Avenue of the Americas, New York, NY 10020

Lott, Bret.
A dream of old leaves / by Bret Lott.
p. cm.
ISBN 0-671-03821-4
I. Title
[PS3562.0784D74 1989b]
813'.54—dc20 90-12620
CIP

First Washington Square Press trade paperback printing January 1991

10 9 8 7 6 5 4 3 2

WASHINGTON SQUARE PRESS and colophon are registered trademarks of Simon & Schuster Inc.

Printed in the U.S.A.

Contents

Why is it I have come to think of you without

a history or vision or the dreadful tow

of things that moved us and the way we went

out into the real world full of innocence,

passion, and mortality? I don't know.

But things happen every day here.

We could all be alive tomorrow.

Thomas Lynch

"Learning Gravity"

A Dream of Old Leaves

"Daddy," his son whispered, and Paul shot open his eyes. "Daddy, I had a dream."

His son stood next to the bed, only a shadow in the dark of the bedroom, but Paul knew the shadow, the outline of the head; the hair, he could make out in the thin light from the night-light in the hall, stuck up in places like strands of twisted wire. He could see his neck, too, the soft curve of it down to David's shoulders. "Daddy?" the boy whispered.

Paul rolled over onto his back and touched his wife lying next to him, her arm and shoulder warm with sleep.

"Kate?" he whispered. "Your turn."

She mumbled something he could not make out, and rolled over away from him.

"Daddy?" his son whispered again.

Kate and Paul tried to alternate nights bringing David back upstairs to his room, one night Paul's turn to pick him up, slowly move up the stairs in the dark toward the light of another night-light, this one in the bathroom at the top of the stairs; the next night her turn. But Kate's side of the bed was farthest from the bedroom door, and their son's first stop was always Paul's side.

"Daddy," his son whispered again, "I had a dream that woke me up."

Paul sat up in bed, careful not to wake Kate, though he could not be certain why. It was her turn, after all, but he only let his feet slip out from beneath the quilt and sheet, touch the floor. His son backed up a foot or so and held out his hand, ready, Paul knew, for the ritual of being picked up and carried back to bed. Slowly Paul stood, his eyes nearly closed, his mouth thick and dry.

He hoisted David up, and in their routine—the boy as completely in rhythm as Paul—he settled in on Paul's hip, his legs gently wrapped around Paul's waist, his warm head on Paul's shoulder. His arms were limp, draped over Paul's shoulders so that he could just feel his son's fingertips between his shoulder blades, the touch almost nothing, a simple dance across his skin as David's hands moved, jostled with each step Paul took up the staircase.

David had started sleeping through at ten weeks, a fact Paul and Kate often shared with other parents, proud that their son slept while some infants and toddlers were still waking up one and two and three times a night. One couple they knew had a two-and-a-half-year-old girl who still got up twice a night, though she'd stopped nursing a year ago; her parents, Paul knew, promoted the practice, insisting the child sleep in their own room, the girl in a crib in the corner so that any move she made during the night woke the parents, which in turn, Paul imagined, set off the kid. It had to do with sleep rhythms; he had read in one of their books about how babies, like adults, had their own sleep patterns to work out, and that if parents kept interrupting babies when they came out of sleep during the night, the kids would acclimate themselves to their parents, and neither would get any sleep.

But two months ago, a week or so after his fourth birthday, David had started waking up. The first night Paul and Kate had both awakened to David's whimpering upstairs, his quick breaths and high-pitched but quiet gasps, and Paul had rolled out of bed, stumbled up the stairs, Kate just behind him. The two were strangely silent, Paul thought as they rushed into the room, David sitting Indian-style in the middle of the bed. And just as they reached him, Paul stooping to touch him, Kate's hand reaching out right next to his so that the two touched their son at the same moment, David let out a choked squeal. At that moment Paul wondered if their son's scream might not have been caused by the two of them whirling into the room, ghosts in the midst of the boy's dream as they touched him, spoke his name in gentle, hushed tones. Kate sat on the bed and took him in her arms, Paul still standing, his hand on the boy's head, in his hair, caressing him.

"I had a dream," David had whimpered that first night, and Paul had whispered right away, "What was your dream about?" thinking only that, perhaps, he wanted to talk, and that talking about the dream would help him get it out, forget it.

Kate was slowly rocking the boy, one hand making slow circles on his back. She looked up at Paul, and in the dark he could make out her expression, the eyebrows knotted, the mouth pursed. When she whispered "Shhh," he knew precisely what she was telling him: Don't ask about the dream. Talking will only bring it back.

But David, his face against Kate's shoulder, said, "It's old leaves in my room on the floor," and Paul could only shrug at Kate. He kept his hand on the boy's head, stroking the hair, until a few moments later Kate moved to lay him down. She slowly pulled the sheet and comforter up to his chin.

They watched him for a few moments there in the dark, and then Paul felt Kate's arm around his waist, felt her lean on him. "His first bad dream," she had whispered almost too quietly to hear, her words moving up to him like ghosts themselves, like old leaves scattered across the room, and he had shivered in the darkness. "It's sad," she had whispered.

David woke up every night after that, and for the first few nights they had done the same thing: hurry from bed up to the room, hold David until the whimpering died down. Each night David said, "I had a dream," then Kate laid him back on the bed, his stuffed koala bear under one arm, the sheet and comforter up to his chin, and the boy would fall asleep. Each night they stood next to the bed a moment less, and by the fifth night Kate's arm was no longer around Paul's waist as they looked at him. By the end of the first week they no longer stood over him, but as soon as he was covered up the two of them were headed out the door and down the stairs where, no matter how short a time they had been away, the sheets had become cold, and the two of them would have to nestle into one another to regain what warmth they had had before David had drawn them from sleep.

They debated nightly over what to do: Should they call their pediatrician? A sleep specialist? Put off doing anything for another week or two? And they pored over their books, reading more about children's dreams, about sleep and about waking up in the middle of the night: six books said to let the baby cry, five said to comfort the child immediately. They tried both tactics, but neither seemed to work. David still cried whether they let him sit by himself or took him up in their arms, and Paul and Kate, both more exasperated than when David had been an infant waking twice a night, woke each morning with bloodshot eyes.

Finally, after a month of his waking up, Kate and Paul lay in bed, listening to the whimpering. "This hurts," she said to the ceiling, but she made no move to push back the sheets and start up the stairs.

Paul knew what she meant: It was as if the two of them had suddenly sided with the books that said let the child cry, get back to his own sleep patterns. From where Paul lay, he could see the red numbers of the digital clock on the nightstand, and he started keeping track of how long David would cry. He whispered, "Three-eighteen."

Kate said nothing. She didn't move, and Paul said, "Three-nineteen."

Twelve minutes later—the longest, Paul knew, they had ever let him go, each minute seeming a day long—David finally stopped, the whimpering dying away to silence. Paul gave the quiet two minutes more before he moved onto his back, tried to see Kate in the darkness. Her head was turned to him, and he could see a smile on her face. "We did it," he whispered.

And then he had felt a tap at his shoulder, quickly turned to see the shadow of his son standing next to the bed, his hair as unruly as ever, one hand to his eyes and rubbing away. "I had a dream that woke me up, Daddy," David had said.

Paul made it to the top of the stairs, David already asleep, his cheek on Paul's shoulder, the arms on his back even more limp. His own eyes still nearly closed—he had, he realized, almost acclimated himself to this new sleep pattern—Paul went into the boy's room and to his bed. Just before laying him down amid his stuffed animals and the bunched-up sheet and comforter, Paul gave his son a small kiss, his lips touching David's wild hair.

He laid his son on the bed, and then, just as he was pulling back the sheet and comforter, David whispered, "I have to go to the bathroom, Daddy."

Paul felt the smile leave him, his face giving over to some piece of small anger. He said, "But you went already. When Mommy and Daddy went to bed."

"I have to go," David said, and on the edge of his whispered voice Paul could hear the movement toward crying, toward tears that he knew would be hard to stop in the middle of the night.

He put his hands on his hips, closed his eyes tight for a moment, then let out a heavy sigh. "Let's go," he said, and held out his hand.

Once at the toilet, David pulled up his pajama top and tucked it under his chin. Everything in the small bathroom—the towels on the rack, the dinosaur shower curtain, the toothbrush holder and cup, even himself and his son—was bathed in a hazy brown thrown by the night-light next to the medicine cabinet, that brown seeming so bright in the room that both Paul and David were squinting, David leaning against the toilet, Paul next to him, pulling down the boy's pajama bottoms.

Then David peed, and Paul watched through eyes still half-closed as his son stood before the toilet, the sound of water into water filling the room. When the sound had stopped, Paul watched for his son to give the one last shiver, his whole body momentarily filled with a quick tremble that signaled he was through.

And David did shiver, just as he had every night Paul had brought him to the bathroom, and there was something in the fullness of that movement, his son quivering just an instant, that reminded him of being a boy himself, and of nights like this one when his own father took him to the bathroom, his father's hair wild, too, his pajama bottoms loose and baggy as he stood next to Paul and waited, he remembered, for him to finish.

David let the pajama top fall from his chin, and Paul leaned over, pulled the bottoms up to his waist, then picked him up again, carried him back to the room.

This time David merely rolled onto his side, took the koala bear in his arms, and settled his cheek against the pillow, Paul pulling the sheet and comforter to his chin. The room seemed immensely darker now, and David's features, his face and ears and his hair, were lost to him. Beneath him was merely a child, his own, under covers, already moving into sleep.

Paul turned and started back to the door, imagined Kate in bed downstairs. At least the sheets would still be warm, he thought.

Then he heard noises, something he could not name coming from somewhere he could not see, and for a moment he thought he had imagined the sound, had dreamed while walking through his own home in the middle of the night. He stopped, listened, heard what seemed to him a scratching of sorts, a rustle and static break of sound from outside his son's bedroom window.

He went to the window and pulled back curtains that in daylight were decorated with colorful teddy bears, but which in the darkness held only gray shapes and silhouettes.

Paul saw outside first the half-moon, bright and crisp, so bright that he could see no stars. Next he saw the trees behind their house, limbs filled with moonlight, each moving in its own rhythm to the breeze out there. Movement, he realized, that made the sounds he heard: leaves against leaves against leaves, sounds that entered the room like ghosts and fell into the ears of his son to give him dreams of old leaves.

Paul turned from the window, still holding the curtain to let in moonlight. He could see his son in the bed, and he thought of the courage a boy might need to make his way down a set of stairs in a dark house, while up in his room stirred sounds that brought him bad dreams. And the light of a starless, moonlit night made him remember an evening months ago, long before the dreams had begun, when he and Kate and David had gone out to dinner rather than face an empty kitchen at the end of a long workday, Kate's boss riding her with a specs deadline, two of Paul's clients backing out of appointments at the last minute. They had picked up David at the day-care center, then driven straight to Quincy's, where David had insisted he push his own tray and knife and fork and spoon along the railing toward a cashier who asked him how he would like his kid steak cooked. "Hot," he had answered.

Afterward, the sun just beneath the horizon so that only two or three stars shone through the blue above, the three started across the parking lot toward their car.

Suddenly David stopped, let go of Paul and Kate's hands. His feet set apart as far as possible, he made a fist with one hand, pointed his arm straight and stiff before him, his fist jutting out into space.

"Mommy, Daddy," he said, and they had both stopped, turned

to their child in the middle of a restaurant parking lot. "There's danger out there," he said, "and I'm going there."

He posed a moment longer, his face with a forced grimace, and then David seemed to fly apart, his arms gone mad, his legs taking him in wild circles, his head shaking back and forth, eyes open wide, his crazy smile of teeth together and lips parted.

"Whoa," Paul had laughed, and Kate had said, "You nutbox," and then they had done their best to steer him toward their car, and toward the short ride back home, where they would bathe him and dry him and brush his teeth and read to him a bedtime story, either *Make Way for Ducklings* or *Hop on Pop*, his two favorite books.

Paul let the curtain fall, and the room grew dark once again. In the darkness he thought of David's words, the truth uttered by a four-year-old for whom facing danger and heading into it meant, perhaps, nothing more than looking to the first stars in the sky of a restaurant parking lot and putting a fist into the air.

And he thought again of when he was a child, back to when danger meant to Paul looking beneath his bed before going to sleep. He remembered his father coming into his bedroom in the middle of a night just like this one, just like any other night, still wearing only his pajama bottoms, his hair still tangled with sleep, his eyes squinting back the light as he switched it on. He remembered his father slowly, patiently lifting the mattress and box spring, then dismantling Paul's bed frame and moving everything underneath it out to show him once and for all that nothing was there. The frame in pieces on the floor, the mattresses on their sides and leaned against the wall, his father had put his hands on his hips, slowly shaken his head, and whispered, "Nothing. See?"

Paul tried to remember any nights after that one when he had been afraid of what was beneath the bed, and he could find nothing in his memory, only nights filled with sleep, and the good knowledge that, in fact, beneath his bed lay only a couple of board games and a flat, long box filled with his winter clothes.

He went to David's bed. Gently he pulled back the comforter and sheet, and eased himself under the covers, amazed at the warmth given by his son, Paul's feet cold but already growing warmer as he pushed them down to the foot of the bed. There was not much room, but then David, still in his sleep, moved closer to the wall, giving his father just enough room to fit beside him.

In California

When I wake up, my grandmother is already playing solitaire in the kitchen, the slap of the cards as she lays them on the Formica tabletop bringing me from sleep. Then she begins to sing, her comforting voice soft and dark as I piece together the words to "Somewhere My Love." And, I remember, today is the day.

She is nearly blind, and the cards she uses have huge numbers, the symbols just as huge, and there seems something sad about the loss of the one-eyed Jack or the Queen of Hearts to just a huge *J* or *Q* with a giant spade next to it. But, I realize, the value is in the game itself; she plays solitaire and sings each morning, passing time until my ex-actor grandfather gets back from wherever he is. Saturdays, Sundays, and Wednesdays it's the swap meets at the drive-in in Artesia, two or three other mornings each week the empty lot next to the Dales Market on Sepulveda, where he parks his van, opens wide the doors, and hangs out for sale the caftans he makes in the garage.

I was discharged from the Navy two weeks ago, and I've been camped here ever since. Although I was born in California, I live—or did live—with my parents up in Salt Lake City; my father transferred there only a month after I was born.

My birthday fell only five months after their wedding day, which might give a clue as to the status I was afforded around the house while growing up, and when I ran away the first time when I was fifteen, it was simply to give them a head start: I'd spent enough nights lying awake and watching out my window the black silhouettes of the Wasatch rising up into stars, while listening to my parents' calm arguments, their mutual resolve each time to divorce and get it over with once I was out of high school. The second time I ran away was my eighteenth birthday, the day I joined the Navy to See The World.

But they still haven't finished the job before them, though I've been in the Navy for four years, and so here I am. I was a machinist's mate, and I figure I'll stay down here in L.A. for a while, see what turns up in San Pedro. There's been nothing so far, but I'm not going back there, back to where I once lived.

The problem, though, is where to go now.

I hear her slap down the cards again, and sit up on the couch, my legs tangled in the sleeping bag. Like every morning so far, I have to blink three or four times, look around the living room, take stock of where I am.

It takes only a moment or so. There is the wood-grain television console against the far wall, big as a coffin; to my right is a pair of velvet recliners, burgundy; above them is a pair of swag lamps, turquoise shades with gold pull tassels. On the left wall is a player piano, heaped atop it dozens of long, skinny boxes, in each box a song, tunes like "Cactus Polka" and "Around the World (I Search for You)."

But what makes me *know* where I am every morning is the evidence of my grandfather's past money-making projects: On the console is a gold-painted plaster statue of a naked cherub, a bowl of grapes on its shoulder; on the small end table between the recliners sits a blue and turquoise and violet feather flower arrangement. I have only to see the statue, the arrangement of feathers, to realize I'm not on the U.S.S. *Denver* anymore, but here at Grandma and Grandpa's, with a full day ahead of me.

I stand, fish from my duffel bag at the foot of the couch a pair of shorts, fold up the sleeping bag, stow it next to the duffel.

Grandma sits at the kitchen table wearing one of the caftans, this one giant white lilies on a purple background. Cards are spread all over the table, three of them held up to her face, her eyes squinted nearly shut. This is my mother's mother, a woman who lost one eye to glaucoma twenty years ago, the other eye left with only 5 percent vision. She's told me stories of trying to raise my mother with headaches lasting months, weeks spent in bed, while somewhere a doctor continued to diagnose her pain as a problem with her glasses. Now, when she walks through the house, it's along walls, one hand touching all the way through.

Her arms are pale and thick, her face wrinkled and white, her mouth too red. Sometimes she seems *too* pale, but I imagine that's because of the caftan material and the blond-gone-gray of her hair. And, too, the fact she leaves her home only twice a week, each time for a walk to the liquor store at the corner. My grandfather on one arm, her white-and-red-tipped cane in the other hand, she buys three cartons of Benson and Hedges Gold.

But she sees things, in her way. Yesterday morning I stood in the kitchen, the cupboards open, and pulled down a box of Special K. She said, "That's for your grandfather. There's not enough of that left for the two of you," and I looked at her, a good fifteen feet away. She was hunched over the cards in her hand, eyes squinted as hard as always.

She brought the cards even closer to her face, held them flat to catch light from the fixture above the table. "What the hell do you make of this card, Gordy?" she said. "Is this a seven or a nine?"

This morning is no different from the last thirteen: I move past her at the table, a cigarette at her lips; to her left, next to the spread of cards, is her leather cigarette case and lighter and beanbag ashtray all placed exactly where she wants them. I pause a moment, take up the cigarette case and shake one out, say, "Mind?" She smiles, the cigarette bobbing up as she lays down a black three on a red nine.

"Just know that when you strike it rich," she says, and lays down the two cards left in her hand, takes up three more from the stack in her other, "you can buy me a goddamn boxful for my birthday. A whole case of Benson and Hedges. That would be nice."

By this time I'm already staring up at the open cupboards, my cigarette already lit; I borrowed her lighter as well. There on the shelf sits the box of Special K. I turn to her.

She shrugs, says, "So he didn't have time for breakfast. He said he had to meet Rosa early, then set up at Dales. He'll be back around one. So you go ahead and finish that off." She slaps down one card on the rows before her, then the second one in her hand, then the third, and she stops. "And don't you worry about today being today. Just don't you worry." Then, with her eyes still squinted, she leans back in the chair, scans the cards, takes one long pull on the cigarette. I can see the cigarette burning down as she draws in deeper than any Navy man I can remember. She can ash a cigarette in two easy pulls.

She brings the stub from her mouth, without looking at it taps three inches into the tray next to the lighter. There's not a trace of smoke as she gives a little laugh, says, "I won."

The business about today being today refers to my personal goals for life after the Navy. When the *Denver* put in in San Diego, I was not surprised to see, as I stood on deck in my dress blues scanning the crowd on the wharf, a caftan of yellow orchids on a sea of fuchsia, my grandmother wearing dark glasses. In one hand she had that cane, next to her the tan face and white hair of my impossibly handsome grandfather.

I couldn't help but smile, wave back to them amid the dozens of other people down there, because my grandparents were the ones I ran *to* when I was fifteen, two days of walking and riding from Salt Lake to L.A. The first night I spent beneath an overpass near St. George, hail the size of lemons pounding down on either side of me, the next night beneath an overpass outside Barstow, the heat off the high desert too heavy for sleep. When I showed up at their door they didn't seem surprised. "You have arrived!" my grandfather said as he swung open the front door, and then he laughed, one hand on his hip. My grandmother slowly moved toward the door, one hand to the wall of the foyer. "What child is this?" she sang. Then she laughed, too.

I'd cried, me hungry and broken, these two laughing at me.

On the ride home from San Diego I'd told them of my goals: to get at least a tight lead on a job in L.A. within the next two weeks, to let my hair grow out, to see at least two new movies a week, to shower alone. The latter ones were, of course, attainable, but if I didn't get a lead on a job in two weeks, I told them as we headed through the grass wasteland of Camp Pendleton, then I didn't know what I would do.

Conversation the whole way home was empty of my parents, but by that time—seven years since running from a dead house—that was fine with me, just as welcome as the green hills of San Juan Capistrano in the distance up ahead.

I'd gone on then to let Grandma and Grandpa know precisely what I'd done on this last cruise, SEAPAC, my third one since enlisting: how once again I'd read my brains out, this trip everything from *Moby Dick* to *The Sacred and the Profane* to *The Machinist's Guide to Valve-Bore Maintenance*; told them of the narrow cans of beer sold in Yokohama and Pusan; told them of the small fire in the engine room when I'd been on duty, and the broken nose I'd gotten when I'd been kicked in the face by the man on the ladder up before me.

"Just look at this," I'd said, leaning toward my grandpa and pointing to the new bump at the bridge of my nose. "Can you see that?" I said, and he had only laughed, his eyes never leaving the road. From behind me my grandma said, "That looks horrible," and I'd turned to face her, saw her with her glasses still on, her mouth and forehead and the lines beside her eyes screwed up into her perpetual squint. "But it's hardly noticeable," she'd said.

Grandpa laughed even harder, but then he stopped, and the inside of the car was silent for the first time since leaving San Diego.

"Your mother called," he said, breaking the quiet, and Grandma leaned forward in the back seat, said, "Earl," his name meant to carry some significant weight. But my grandfather sensed nothing, or, if he did, acted right through the moment. He said, "She told me to inform you that she and Gordon just couldn't get the time off from work, that her bank wouldn't allow it, that your father's office was swinging into season now. They both send their love."

"Earl," she said again, and he looked into the rearview mirror, said her name: "Saralee."

"Thanks for the info," I'd said, and let it drop there.

Near ten o'clock Grandma stops the solitaire, satisfied at winning her quota of five games. She wins at solitaire more often than anyone else I know.

I have gone over the L.A. *Times* four times by now, turning up the same nothing I've seen for two weeks, when the front door bangs open. My grandfather enters, shouts, "Sons of bitches all!" in what I know is his most practiced best; he is still an actor. "Sons of bitches all!" he shouts again, and though he hasn't startled me in the least—the few times I spent here when I was a child got me used to his practical jokes: the blast of the radio on after you'd just nodded off in the car; the pinch of a fingernail on the forearm, his cigarette between his fingers so that for a moment you thought he'd burned you with the tip—still I oblige him, let the newspaper in my hands drop, give the cigarette at my lips a quick shiver.

But my grandma only shouts, "Earl, knock it off!" He pauses in the middle of the living room, seems to draw himself up, his eyes fixed on the woman in the burgundy recliner before him. A game show plays on the television, for a moment the room filled with only the sound of bells ringing, of a woman's mad scream at having won a roomful of furniture, and I wonder just how long my grandparents have fought this way, their way of life so opposite to my parents'.

Earl and Saralee's only wedding picture hangs in the hall between bedroom and bathroom. In it he wears a white dinner jacket, my grandmother a gray dress. They are smiling, but in my grandmother's face there is something forced, her teeth maybe clenched too tight, and every time I pass the picture I wonder if even then she wasn't already feeling the small crack of pain, glaucoma setting in even before her honeymoon night.

Earl's smile is better rehearsed than Saralee's, chiefly due to the Republic Pictures movie he was about to work on then: *Thirteen Fighting Men*, a movie in which he gets hung in the first three minutes. All you can see of him are his dangling feet once the trapdoor has been thrown open. Other roles he's had include that of a Western Union man handing a telegram to John Wayne, and the town doctor in one episode of "The Andy Griffith Show," his part cut before airing because the program had run too long. The latest work he's done, maybe ten or twelve years ago, was a Foremost Milk commercial. In it he plays a carpenter nailing shingles on a roof, pausing to down a quart of milk. A few moments later a refrigerator opens up in a kitchen somewhere, and he reaches in for yet another quart. You can see him clearly: he's right there, reaching between a jar of mayonnaise and a carton of eggs for the milk. But there's no smile on his face, only the determination of a man set on getting milk.

I remember the night I saw him there on our TV in Salt Lake, the startling surprise of my grandfather entering our home through the black-and-white television, his back bent at nailing, his Adam's apple bouncing as he drank straight from the carton.

My mother and father were there, the two of them on the couch and watching the screen intently, as always no words between them. And when the commercial was over, my grandfather, it occurred to me, was already lost to the blank faces of people watching television all across the nation, my parents included.

But for now we are a captive audience here in his living room, and Grandpa says, "Rosa will never again have my business, nor any of the business of my colleagues."

The game show credits roll on the screen too fast to see, and Grandma has no smile, only squints.

"What now?" she says, her head weaving a little, looking for him, I imagine.

"What now?" I say.

"Oh," he says, and the actor lets out his breath. "Caftan material that fat old Mexican promised me. She sold it off to Clara McClaine. That means I'm going to be short for the next couple of weeks. Means, too, any caftans I make will have to be out of that rose-on-white left from last month."

"And what the hell's wrong with that material?" Grandma says. "I've got three made out of it. What's wrong with it?"

"The reason you have three," he says, and now he sits on the couch next to me, throws his arms back and onto the top of the sofa, exhausted and irritated at having to deal with idiots, "is because we can't *give* that hideous pattern away. Makes anyone who wears it look like white whales tattooed with dead flowers." He pauses, glances at me and smiles. "Of course," he says, and clears his throat, "present company excluded."

Grandma turns to the set, still squints, holds her head as though the commercial playing there were more important than we could ever know. "Just go straight to hell, would you, Earl?" she says.

I spent one month here the first time I ran away. Grandpa was full swing into the plaster statue phase; feather flowers came once I was on my way to Yokohama. The inside of the garage was filled with rubber molds and sacks of plaster, and the first five days I was here I sat and watched him mix water and plaster in a vat, pour it into molds for cherubs, Grecian women in tunics fallen to reveal round, full breasts, even an occasional unicorn or Head of Nefertiti. Then he would let the filled molds dry in the afternoon heat of the garage. Later that evening the plaster, once the rubber mold was peeled away like a thick layer of dead skin, was warm, and Grandpa would execute the finer touches: with a small piece of wet chamois he would dab at the seam in the plaster where the two halves of the mold had met, then he'd fill in any small holes or irregularities in the statue. He knew what he was doing, the seam disappearing with the smallest touch of the chamois, the pockmarked breast of a Greek woman smooth, unblemished, with the touch of a penknife and a bit of wet plaster.

The next morning we would go back into the garage, dark and cool now. Grandpa would break out the spray paint, put the statue on a potter's wheel, and lacquer it over with metallic gold or silver. Then he would stand back from it, his hands on his hips, on his face the actor's scowl no matter how perfect the cherub seemed to me. Satisfied, he would place it among the other statues on the shelves against the back wall of the garage, waiting for the next swap meet.

All that time, Grandma played solitaire inside the house. On occasion we might hear her beautiful voice, fine and clear enough to have come from some easy-listening station, moving through "Que Sera, Sera" or "A Taste of Honey" accompanied by the player piano, or hear her shout at the television, "The car! Take the car, you idiot!"

After six days of watching him work, Grandpa let me try spray-painting a unicorn whose horn had broken off while the mold was being removed. Halfway through, the head and front legs covered in gold, I heard the phone ring inside. We both glanced up at each other, then looked back at the work at hand.

A few minutes later the door at the back of the garage opened, the dark room flooded with midmorning light. I turned, stopped spraying. Grandma stood in the doorway, the silhouette of a woman in an old housedress, one hand just touching the doorjamb.

"Gordy?" she called out.

"Right here," I said. Grandpa hadn't turned to her. From the corner of my eye I could see he was staring at the statue, his head moving one way and the other, assessing how well I'd done so far.

"Gordy, it's your mother."

I put the can down on the potter's wheel, wiped my hands on my pants legs, started toward her. "She's on the phone right now?" I said, and I thought I might have felt on my face the beginnings of a smile.

Grandma put up a hand to stop me. Her hand hovered before her, moved back and forth as if she were touching the air.

"No," she said, and I stopped, her pale fingers inches from my chest. She said, "No, she called and left a message. She said she wanted to make sure you were all right." She reached toward me, and I felt her fingers just touch my chest.

I closed my eyes. "That's all?" I said, and waited for an answer.

From behind me I heard the sound of the ball bearing inside the paint as my grandfather started shaking the can.

"Come on," he said, "I see a few runs in the job here. You got to make your sweeps smooth and easy. Just smooth and easy," and I heard the hiss of metallic gold out of a can.

Grandma blinks off the TV now, moves the recliner to upright. "Let's go for cigarettes now," she says.

"Get those godforsaken coffin nails yourself!" he shouts with the bravado he's had as long as I have known him, and suddenly I am standing up from the couch, heading toward the front door. "I'll take her," I say, though I've never taken her before. It's just that today is The Day, and there is nothing in the newspaper for me.

Grandma is at the door a few moments later, her red-tipped cane at the ready, dark glasses on, and Grandpa yells, "And I'm glad to see you up and moving for once, Gordon the Second. Atrophy kills!"

"It's the caftan material," she says to me once we are on the driveway. "He'll grab any opportunity he can to go ranting around the house." She holds the cane perpendicular to the ground, the bottom tip never touching earth. Her posture is impeccable, her neck straight and sure, and as we make our way onto the sidewalk, I see too clearly I am still a boy who's run from home, away to his grandparents' house.

We make it to the corner, her left arm looped in mine, before us the midday traffic of Sepulveda Boulevard. Though I've passed here any number of times, have known that Hanshaw's Liquor Mart II is where she buys her cigarettes, I see only then that the place is directly across Sepulveda. There is no crosswalk before us, only four lanes of fast cars and a double yellow line.

With my arm I begin to steer her to the right and the traffic light at the intersection one hundred yards or so away, but she draws to a dead stop.

She says, "Where the hell are you going?" She wrestles her arm free of mine, grasps the cane with both hands, the tip still inches above ground.

"Down to the light," I say. "And then across. Right?"

"Hell, no," she says, and she smiles, the wrinkles nearly gone, and I can see the young woman in the wedding picture in her hall.

"Watch," she says, and turns to the curb, inches up to it. She stands there a moment, then extends the cane out before her, angled down to meet the pavement. She taps it hard in a perfect rhythm, the tip making an arc from left to right and back again, and she steps off.

I reach for her, but she says over her shoulder, "Back in a minute." Cars everywhere roar to a stop, and I watch my grandmother in a purple caftan covered with huge white lilies cross Sepulveda Boulevard without hesitating a moment.

She makes it to the sidewalk across the street, and she moves slowly again, the cane no longer touching ground but hovering above it, just as before. The door into the place is only a few feet away from her, but still it takes a minute for her to make it, one hand out in front of her until a thin woman with blue-black hair and thick glasses appears in the doorway, smiles, and calls out "Saralee," so loudly I can hear it over the traffic between us, all cars back to well above speed limit. Grandma disappears inside.

When she comes back out, she's carrying a paper sack, inside of which, I know, are three cartons. She moves just as slowly as before, until she reaches the curb. She touches the cane to the street again, and the world seems to halt around her, cars freezing as she taps out the ground before her. Then she is next to me, her arm looped in mine again, and she is pulling me back down their street, me too stunned to say a thing.

"Not bad for a loudmouth blind grandma," she says, and I can only nod in agreement. "I won't let Earl take me across that street. It's the only thing I have left, I think," and she goes quiet for a moment. "You should hear us bitch and moan at each other all the way down here," she starts up again, "and every time it's over whether or not he'll let me cross alone. Him and his frustrated actor business, flailing his arms everywhere, but I just go right across, and he hasn't stopped me a single day yet. By the time I get back, he's still steamed up, and we march on off into the sunset bitching and moaning away."

I haven't yet said a word, and we are quiet for a while until she says, "It's not that they don't love you." Then, a few moments later, a few feet farther away from the sounds of traffic behind us, she says, "But then how do I know that's the truth?" and she stops walking.

She looks for me, reaches her fingers up to my face and touches me. "I love you," she says. "You know that, don't you?"

I nod, her fingers still at my cheek, and I say, "I love you too," surprised at how the words sound out here on the street, the silence that follows them. And because of how much I fear that silence, the dead sound around us, I say, "Sing for me."

"What?" she says.

"Sing for me," I say, and I give her hand a small squeeze.

She stops squinting a moment, the wrinkles gone somehow. The street is quiet, no cars anywhere. Then she smiles, and with no more hesitation than that she begins to sing: "Evening summer breeze, warbling are the meadowlarks, moonlight in Vermont . . ."

I close my eyes, and suddenly she stands before a big band, the smiling maestro's fluid hands only a vague imitation of her beautiful voice. She has on a turquoise flounced gown as she sings on: "Telegraph cables sing down the highway, travel each bend in the road—"

By the time we make it to the driveway she's gone twice through "Moonlight in Vermont," once through "Misty," and is in the middle of "Route 66." The things she's lost since the picture in the hall—the blond hair, the girlish figure—don't matter. What matters is that the woman next to me, posture still perfect, gives to the hot summer air around us a voice clear and simple.

But when we are halfway up the drive, I look up, see Grandpa standing at the open door. One hand is on the knob, in the other a fistful of mail. On his face is no expression, and I realize the look he gives might actually be who he is, the real Earl behind the failed actor.

We make it to the three concrete steps up to the door, and I say to him, "What now?"

Grandma turns to me, unaware, I believe, that Grandpa stands before us. She says, "Why not 'Someone to Watch Over Me'?"

"Mail call," Grandpa says, his voice flat and dead. "You got a letter."

Grandma looks up at him. "From?" she asks, but there is no suspense in her voice, only dread somehow.

He says nothing, pulls from the wad of bills and fliers in his hand a small thank-you note of a letter.

But I only hold the envelope in my hand, stare at handwriting familiar yet foreign on the front of it, and at the small return address sticker on the upper left corner. The name and numbers there mean something, I am certain, but as I stare at them they become only bits of ink on a self-adhesive strip. I don't know anyone there, don't even know where the hell Salt Lake City is, and I look first to Grandpa, then to Grandma, then to the envelope again.

I fold it in half, and half again, a small square of white paper in my hand. I shove it deep into my back pocket, hoping I might not remember where I put it later on.

A moment of silence again passes before us, the quiet so great I hear the rush of blood through me, and then Grandpa's hand is on my shoulder, and he leads me up the steps, my feet moving on their own. I turn to Grandma, still on the driveway.

"Don't worry about me," she says, and again I am amazed, wondering what she can see and what she cannot. "I'm fine."

"Today is the day," Grandpa says as he leads me through the living room, my duffel still stowed beneath the end table at the foot of the couch, in it everything I own, equipment for whatever start seems suddenly close. "Come with me."

We move through the kitchen, through the laundry room, and out onto the small porch in the backyard, down three more steps and to the back door into the garage.

Then we are inside, the air enormously cooler, and he clicks on the light to reveal three industrial sewing machines, rolls and rolls of rose-on-white material stacked around the room. Hanging from rungs wired to rafters are caftans, dozens of them, some beige with yellow carnations, others crimson with blue dahlias, but most of them in that rose-on-white pattern.

His hand is on my shoulder again, and he weaves me through piles of cardboard boxes and past two of the sewing machines to the third one. He sits me down on the stool before it.

"The other two are temperamental," he says, "maybe just a little too much so. This one here is reliable, won't skip a beat and sew your finger right into the hem of the dress some old woman will slip over her head. You sure as hell don't want that," he says, and then he laughs, slaps my back in a gesture that, I suddenly realize, might be real.

I turn to him, see he is already kneeling at one of the boxes behind me. He pulls out a huge piece of material, his face all concentration, lips drawn tight and closed. What we are about to do matters to him.

He lays the material over one arm, with his free hand reaches beneath the machine top and flicks a switch, and a small light on the machine flashes on, a soft whir begins.

"We'll just practice right now," he says, and folds one edge of the material onto itself, leans over me to drop the material in my lap, the colors brighter now because of the light from the machine.

He puts his arms around me from behind, places his hands on the platform beneath the needle and machinery, and says, "Feel around with your foot. There's a pedal down there."

Then the back door opens up. For a moment I feel as though I am only fifteen again, newly run from home, and we both turn to the light.

Once again I see only her silhouette, but once she closes the door behind her I see that she's changed from the purple-and-lily caftan into one made from the same rose-on-white I hold now.

"I don't give a damn if I *do* look like a beached and tattooed whale," she says. "I like this pattern." She moves toward us, her hands to either side of her, slowly maneuvering through the obstacles around her. Before she reaches us, Grandpa turns from her back to the machine, his arms around me once again, his hands on the material.

"Good for you," he says loud enough for her to hear. Then, quieter, he says, "Find the pedal?"

"Yes," I say, my foot on something square beneath the table.

"Okay," he says, and slides the edge of the material beneath the needle. "Now press down slowly on it, not too hard. Slowly."

I press down with the tip of my shoe, the touch tentative, near nothing. The needle moves almost imperceptibly down toward the material, and I press harder.

The needle goes wild then, shoots the material through, the whir of the machine gone to a mad whine, and before I can let up my foot, Grandpa yells, "Easy! Easy! Come on now!"

Grandma is next to us now, and I feel a blush come over me, close my eyes a moment.

"Easy," she whispers, and I open my eyes to the machine, my foot on the pedal. I ease it down, let the material feed itself through, perhaps too slowly right now, the needle hesitating each time before slipping down into the material. But the line leading out is as straight as I can make it, and there seems some direction in this movement, though what I am beginning I cannot say.

Crazy

It is after midnight, and I lie here in bed, my arms up over my head, holding on to the headboard. I'm staring at the ceiling, at the dresser, at the fan in the window. My husband Albert is next to me, asleep, lightly snoring the way he does, a sound like spit down the back of his throat, moving around with each breath in. He could be dead, except for that sound in the back of his throat.

Then I hear *click, click* from somewhere in the house. *Click, click* again, like metal on metal. For a moment I think a train is going by. The tracks are at the end of the street, up on a raised platform of dirt, our street dead-ending there. But I don't feel the rocking that comes with the train, no gentle motion through the house.

I hear *click, click* again.

What I do is this: I sit up in bed, listen. I hear it again, get out of bed, and walk out into the hall. The sound could be anything in the house: the shower head in the bathroom, the refrigerator, the pipes. Things like this sound are common in our house. It's an old place, and we bought it as a fixer-upper. The ad in the paper had read, "All she needs is a little TLC."

We didn't have a great deal of money. I am a teller at Union National, and Albert works part-time as a stock clerk at Waldbaum's. When we had finally decided to buy a house three years ago, we pored over the classifieds for months, looking for homes that needed TLC or were a Handyman's Dream or needed Finishing Touches.

The living room needs drywall, we need new linoleum in the kitchen, and the hall closet and kitchen need ceilings in them. There are nicks and gashes in the hardwood floors of the bedrooms and hall. The outside of the house should be scraped and painted or, better yet, have that new vinyl siding installed all the way around. But the place is clean. At least we have a house, a *home,* and for that I am thankful.

Click, click. I move down the hall, wishing I'd put on my slippers to avoid splinters in my feet from the nicked-up floor. I go into the bathroom, leaving the light off, and put my hand on the shower head. I shake it; there's no leak here, I think, then whisper, "Nothing."

I go from there to the kitchen. Someone at one time or another scraped a refrigerator across the floor, so that now, even with the lights out, I can see deep furrows on the floor, the linoleum dug down to black resin.

The sound isn't the refrigerator either, and then I hear *click, click* again, coming from the living room. I make my way out there, into the room in which drywall needs to be hung, the room in which you can see the studs right there, and the tarpaper behind the frame boards. You can see the pipes going to and from the kitchen and bathroom. We've hung a couple of pictures over the pipes, but it seems that only draws attention to things washing through there. Albert disagrees with me. The pictures were his idea.

The pipes are making no noise, and I hear it again, coming from outside the window.

The window is up, and I pull a curtain back. My next-door neighbor is out there with a flashlight. *Click, click* I hear. That's the sound. He's out there working on his car, tightening something on his Chevette, his elbow working up and down. The flashlight lies on the ground, silhouetting him hunched up against the car, and throws weird shadows across the neighborhood.

I should have known. This man is crazy. He babies his car to no end. I've watched him out there past midnight, just like tonight, washing the thing. I've watched him other nights wax it, fool with the stereo, change the tires. He changes the oil once a month, always at night.

I know he works days from eight to five. I've seen him leave for work, always in a three-piece suit, always carrying a briefcase. He and his wife live alone in that big old yellow house next door. Other than that, all I know about him is that he's out there most nights after midnight, working on his car, making noises that keep me awake.

I sit on the couch, start thinking about the crazy things I put up with, starting right here and now with those cheap prints hung over the pipes, and with that man in the driveway. *Click* I hear again. I think about how clean this place is, how I can go to any point in the house, even to the bare studs over there, and run my finger along the top of one. There wouldn't be a speck of dust. I have my mother to thank for this fact.

I think of her, and the first thing that comes to mind is a spring day, me a little girl standing on our front porch, my mother out on the front lawn with a vacuum cleaner. She was vacuuming up all the birdseed that had fallen from my father's feeder.

"Goddamn seeds," she said. "Goddamn feeder, goddamn birds." She looked up from the lawn, saw me watching her, and snapped off the vacuum. She yelled, "Your father and his birds. That crap seed gets into the lawn, who knows what weed circus will grow up out here."

My father came out onto the porch. He limped down the stairs, his leg brace banging loudly on each step, and then calmly, coolly refilled the feeder from a bag of seed he held in his hand. My mother turned the vacuum on, swept back and forth, back and forth, as though my father never existed.

I grew up listening to my father tell me the story of how he had lost use of his leg in Korea when he had fallen on a land mine and saved a dozen buddies. Mother at work, the two of us would sit in the kitchen with the fan in the window, and he would tell me again how he had been at Pork Chop Hill and had fallen and had saved them. He told me other war stories, awful stories about blood and guns and smoke, and I believed him, even after Mother would come home from work and run us into the living room, shouting after us that I shouldn't listen to my father's lies, that he'd lied since the day she'd met him. She never explained what she meant by his telling lies, never felt the need, I guess, to elaborate on that point. Father would hobble into the living room, fall face down on the couch and we'd laugh. Mother stayed in the kitchen and undressed, taking off the smock and skirt she wore as a uniform. She took off her slip, unhooked her hose, then stood there in her long-line bra and underpants, flapping her arms in front of the fan, all the while yelling, "Lies, lies he's telling you." With all the shades up, she would then vacuum, mop, dust every day.

When I was twelve, I watched my dad die of lung cancer, watched him change in six months from an overweight, happy man of thirty-five to an emaciated one of eighty. His leg brace had at one time been a snug fit, but by the time he was finally admitted to a hospital, the brace rattled and clanked as he moved through the house like a ghost.

After the funeral my mother and I sat alone in our house for the first time. We were in the living room, and I started talking about him, about the stories he told me, about his being a hero in Korea.

"What?" my mother said. She blinked, looked at me with her head tilted. She was sitting on the sofa across from me, there in her bra and underpants. She had taken off her clothes the minute the last mourner had left. "What did you say?"

"I said I'm so proud my daddy saved those men in Korea." I pulled my legs up under me, glad I had feeling in both of them.

My mother laughed, slapped the couch with her sweaty palms. "That's a good one. Oh, that's a good one," she laughed. She wiped her eyes, leaned her head back on the sofa, took a deep breath. "Crazy," she said, "I told you he was. He was never in Korea. The closest he got was San Diego."

"His leg," I said, "what about his leg?"

"Hah," she said. "He got hit by a general's jeep when he was crossing the street. He wasn't even on base at the time. It wasn't even on military ground he got injured. I never heard that one before. He never told me that story." I couldn't see her eyes from where I sat, her head back on the sofa, but I knew she was crying. She kept wiping her nose. "Crazy," she said.

After that I started paying more attention to my mother's cleaning techniques, the importance of keeping a refrigerator top dusted, proper screen window washing, me wondering all the time whether it was my mother who was crazy or if it had been my father.

I married Albert when I was a year out of high school. He was about to go into the army, where he knew he would be sent to Vietnam. He'd worried the whole honeymoon about my getting pregnant, neither of us knowing until years later that my womb was locked like some sort of suitcase from day one. I'd hoped and hoped to get pregnant, and when he was finally shipped off to Saigon I waited that month for the blood in my underpants while I dreamed of him, of his sandy hair and mustache, and hoped for letters from him telling me how much he loved me, just as I imagined my parents would have done had my father really been in Korea. My blood came. His letters did not.

Albert came home a sad man. He'd seen a lot, he told me, a lot worse than they were printing in *Life* magazine. He started writing poetry not long after we moved into this shell of a house, and that's why he only works part-time at the market, because he wants to be a poet. He rides his bicycle to work about noon, heads home at three.

His poetry is almost always set in lush, green jungles, the fragrance of wet earth and exotic flowers all around, and there is always blood. I don't know if it's good poetry or bad, but I know it's always about the same things.

One night a few months ago I asked Albert if it was all true, those things he wrote about in his poems. Those green trees and the blood. We were at the dinner table, the refrigerator whirring and clanking, the radiators buzzing like mad in this old house. I waited for his answer.

He had a forkful of food halfway between his plate and mouth. He stopped. He blinked. "Of course," he said. "How could I lie?" He put the food in his mouth.

I took a drink of milk, tipping the glass up so I wouldn't have to look at him, at his sad face. There in the open rafters I saw cobwebs I hadn't gotten the day before.

Right then and there I stood up, set the glass down, then went to the pantry for the broom. I pulled the chair out, centered it beneath where I'd seen that cobweb. I climbed up on the chair and started swinging. I remember thinking, hoping, wishing that someday I'd find out Albert was telling lies, just as my father had, that he'd never been there and was relaying things he'd heard or, better yet, fabricating the whole thing. But there I stood, on the chair, swinging at dust, while my husband calmly ate his dinner, and I knew there was craziness here, too. I wasn't sure where, but it was here.

Click, click I hear again, and I turn to the window, pull back the curtain. He's still out there working on his car; now the hood is up. The flashlight sits on the fender, shining in on the engine, and I can see he's changing the air filter. I know he put in a new one just last week. I was here watching him.

A few minutes later he snaps off the flashlight, gently closes the hood, then collects his three or four tools and the old air filter.

He walks up the driveway onto his porch, reaches with one hand to open the front door, but he waits a second, looks back. For a moment I think he knows I am here watching him, and I duck back from the window. A few seconds later I pull back a corner of the curtain and look out.

He is standing on the porch, facing the car. He has put the tools and things down somewhere, and stands with his arms crossed, rocking back and forth on his heels. He looks at his car a few minutes, and in the darkness I imagine I can see him smiling, proud of the grease and dirt beneath his nails.

Later I get up from the sofa and wander around the house, ending up in the bedroom that would have housed, had I been another woman, our child. It's funny, but this room is the least in need of work. The walls are clean, clear of dings. The ceiling is hung, the window works, the floor is smooth. I slide my feet along the floor like a skater, happy, comforted that there will be no splinters here. I go to my husband's desk, look at the top littered with poems; then I go to the window.

From this window I can see up and down the street: the cars parked there, who is awake and who isn't. It looks as though I were the only one awake in the world, the street is so dark. I lean closer to the window, look out to our porch, and see that Albert has left his bicycle out, fair game for any delinquent walking down the street.

Outside, I take in a deep breath of air. The handlebars are cold in my hand; I put up the kickstand and start walking the bike around to the back. The bike is a three-speed, so as I push it along it makes a *tick, tick* sound on the sidewalk, then on the driveway. Out here in the warm night air that *tick, tick* seems huge. I look over to my neighbor's house to see if he's up and watching.

And there he is, standing at what I had always imagined was a bedroom window. I can't see his face or anything, just a dark silhouette.

I wonder what his wife thinks, if she wonders at all about her crazy husband and his car. I wonder if she is like Albert, serious and asleep right now, oblivious to the fact his barren wife is here in the driveway, pushing along his bike. I wonder what a child between the two of us, me and that car nut, might be like.

I stop the bike, wave up at him, me here in my pajamas pushing a three-speed along.

His shadow disappears from the window.

"Crazy," I whisper, and head back to the garage.

Things That Could Come

He picked Lora up at the office just as he did every night: circled once through downtown traffic around her building, then saw her at the corner, waiting, one hand on the small of her back, the other hung at her side. She held her pocketbook by the strap so that it just touched the sidewalk.

He pulled over, popped open the door. She looked as pregnant as ever. Even her ankles seemed thicker.

Lora fell into the seat, dragged the pocketbook in. John signaled, had the car out and back in traffic before she had gotten the door closed.

She said, "The doctor's office. I can't believe them over there." She let out a heavy breath. Single hairs of her bangs shot up with the air out.

"I called them twice," she said. "I called them to tell them there's something wrong. I don't know. I had some Braxton-Hicks contractions this afternoon and—"

"Why didn't you tell me?" he cut in. He glanced over his shoulder, looked in the side-view mirror. He edged into the next lane, the car behind him laying in on the horn. "Call me?"

"Braxton-Hicks," she said. "Nothing to worry about. I'm only seven months on, you know. I still have nine weeks left."

"They've been born earlier," he said.

"Anyway," Lora said, and let out another breath to let him know she wanted to go on with her story, "I called them three times there at the office. Three times, and no return calls."

"Why call them?" John said, and glanced at her. She had already wheeled the seat back, her head almost even with the bottom edge of the rear window. "You said they were Braxton-Hicks."

"Because," she said, and in that small glance he could see the shine in her eyes. She said, "Because it's regular now," her voice brittle. "Ten minutes apart. And they haven't called me. Not after three times." She swallowed. "The last time I called they said Gunderson's office quit answering phones after five, so I left a message to call me at home. So we have to hurry."

They got home without another contraction. John went ahead and washed his hands with the pumice soap, cleaned the grease out from under his nails and from off the backs of his hands. Then he took out two potatoes, scrubbed them in the sink, started to unwrap the package of thawed chicken. Lora came into the kitchenette then, stood there in her sweat pants and an old red knit shirt of his. She said, "Feel this."

She took one of his hands, placed it on her stomach, and held it there. She had already taken off her makeup, but her lips were red, her cheeks and hands pale.

"Kicking?" John said. He smiled, but he knew by her eyes this was not what she wanted him to feel.

"Push down," she said. "Feel it."

He pressed down on her. The swell beneath the shirt, the skin already pulled taut, felt hard, stiff. Not as it had on other nights when she would wake him from sleep to have him poke and prod, look with his hands for the movement that had awakened her but that he could never find. On those nights the swell had been soft, smooth.

"It's hard," he said. He took his hand away.

"It's started again."

She left him there, and then he heard her on the phone in the other room.

John started in on the breakfast dishes, straightened out the mail—things he didn't want to face when they got home. When *he* got home, he thought.

Lora looked up Gunderson's home phone number, got his answering service. A few minutes later he called and told them to meet him at the hospital.

John and Lora went to the emergency room, then were told by an attendant to follow the brown line back into the hospital to the elevator. They were to go to the third floor, where they would find labor and delivery.

The two followed the line of brown linoleum squares on the floor through double doors that automatically opened for them, then past emergency rooms where people were dressed in clothes that seemed to John horrible there in a hospital: a Hawaiian shirt on a man who lay in a bed, a new cast on his leg; another man who sat on the edge of his bed, shaking his head as he looked at his bare feet, his yellow hair wet, his face gray; a black woman in a neon-green sweatshirt and black pants, passed out on her bed.

They found the elevator, then went up. The door opened to the green-tiled walls of a hallway. They were right there in the wing, two nurses in scrub outfits walking along the corridor, low moans from somewhere to the left, faint cries of babies to the right.

The hallway was immaculate, and John was still in his uniform from the shop. He looked at his hands.

He said, "You look around. You go find where you're supposed to go, and I'll wait in here."

Lora looked both ways down the corridor, then stepped out. She looked back to the left again, turned, said, "I can see a waiting area out there." She pointed. "Through those doors."

He stepped out of the elevator. A few yards down were big double doors with glass windows. Through the windows he could see a room with some furniture, pictures on the walls, windows, flowered wallpaper.

John went to the doors. Before he opened them, though, he turned back to Lora, but she was already down the hall. She stood at an open area—the nurse's station, he imagined—talking to a nurse with red hair high up on her head, the white paper hat tacked on somehow.

The room was empty except for the furniture: a sofa and three overstuffed Naugahyde chairs, a television set against one wall, lamps on a couple of night tables. On one of the tables sat a phone. The sofa, green-and-blue brocade with clear plastic arm covers, sat in the middle of the room and faced the television.

John looked around, saw some magazines on a night table behind the sofa: a *Redbook*, a *Childbirth*, and three old *Newsweeks*. He picked up a *Newsweek*, went to the sofa, flipped through the magazine, looked at news he'd already read at home a month or two before. He stood, went for another one, flipped through this one, too, then got the last *Newsweek*, then the *Redbook*, then the *Childbirth*. He finished all of them in fifteen minutes.

This was it, he knew. This was what they told you about.

He had put the last magazine back with the others and turned on the television when the phone rang. He turned to the sound. He let it ring away, waiting for someone to come through those double doors. But when it rang the seventh or eighth time, he picked up the receiver.

It was Lora. "They've got me hooked up on I.V.," she said. She sounded groggy.

"How did you get me?" he said.

"They gave me the number. Listen," she said, "I'm going to be in here for a while. Gunderson came in and looked me over. Nothing. He told me to hold on and wait for a while."

He closed his eyes. "Do you want me in there?" He crossed one arm, touched his chin to his chest. "In there with you."

She was quiet a second, then said, "Actually, you can come in here and see me for as long as you want, but I'm beat. I want to sleep."

"What do I do?" He still had his eyes closed.

She put her hand over the mouthpiece then, and John could hear the clink of her wedding band against the hard plastic. He heard her say something to someone. "Just go through the doors," she came back on. "We're waiting for you. Just go through."

"I'm filthy," he said.

"Just go," she said. "We're waiting."

She lay on her left side, the johnny tied loosely in the back but covering her well enough. The sheet was bunched up over her feet, her legs from ankle to mid-thigh out in the open. Her eyes were closed, the I.V. needle in the back of her right hand.

He sat in a chair next to the bed, and she opened her eyes.

"This it?" he said.

"Could be." There was some color back in her face now. "Are you ready?" She smiled.

"I don't know," he said. He tried to smile, and put a hand up to her face. My clean hands, he thought. He brushed his fingers across her cheek, and she closed her eyes. She was still smiling. Then she was asleep.

A nurse came in, the same nurse with the red hair and the hat. She stood next to John, took hold of the I.V. tube and stared at it a moment before letting it go. She whispered, "You can wait here if you like."

He looked down at his clothes, his boots. He looked at his hands. He had washed only up to his wrists; above them his arms were dirty, the hair matted in places with grease, and he could see the definite line where his dirty arms stopped and the clean hands took over. He said, "I think I want to wait outside. See what happens."

She smiled down at him, a nurse's smile John knew she gave a thousand times a day. Just the corners of her mouth moving up, her lips never coming apart.

He stood, went for the door, turned. The nurse was already straightening the sheets out over Lora's legs. He said, "You'll call me?"

She stopped, looked up at him, surprised, it seemed, that he was still around.

"Of course."

He went back through the double doors and into the room, still empty. "P.M. Magazine" was on now, a segment about an aerobic exercise class that doubled as a pickup spot. Men in silky running shorts and colored mesh T-shirts were jumping and dancing along with women in spandex leotards and tights and leg warmers.

Then an older couple came into the room. He hadn't seen them come in. They were just there, standing in front of the double doors, looking at the room. The man wore red pants and a white knit shirt and wire-frame glasses. His hair was white, and he had on shiny black pennyloafers. The woman's hair was blond, but John could tell she dyed it, the color just too perfect all the way around. She had on a white silk blouse and a blue skirt. They both could have just come in from a country club.

They didn't say anything, just stood there for a moment, looking. John turned back to the television. A minute or so later they moved, the man heading across the room to one of the chairs against the window, the woman to the far end of the sofa.

John and the woman sat watching the television. Now there was a segment on about a house someone had built entirely of newspapers. Chairs, tables, beds. A piano. Everything of rolled-up newspapers.

The man said, "Mind if I turn off this light?"

The woman and John turned to him at the same time. He had his hand up to the lamp on the night table next to him, his fingers touching the black knob below the shade. His face was blank.

The woman turned to John. She smiled.

"Go right ahead," he said.

The man turned off the light, and the room was almost dark, the only light left coming from another lamp behind them against the far wall. That, and light from the television.

"Thanks," the man said. John looked over at him. He couldn't see the man's face, just the reflection of images from the TV on his glasses, two small blue squares that danced and popped.

John nodded at him, but the man didn't move. He got a cigarette from somewhere, lit it. The tip went bright orange, died down to red.

John turned back to the set, and the woman said, "This your first one?"

He looked at her and felt a smile on his face. "Sure is," he said. "If this is the time. She's only seven months along."

"My," the woman said. She was still looking at the television. "My," she said again. "Seven months. I hope everything works out for you. That she'll be okay." She paused. "I'm sure she'll be okay," she said, and then the man moved in his chair, the Naugahyde crunching with his movement. John glanced over at him. He had turned sideways in the chair, and John could see his profile, the lights of the parking lot through the window behind him. He brought the cigarette to his mouth, dragged on it.

"I hope so, too," John said.

They sat there, no more words between them, until "P.M. Magazine" was over. Just as the credits were coming up the double doors opened. The woman turned to the door. The man was already getting up.

A man came out. He seemed a few years older than John, but he couldn't tell for sure, the room was so dark. This man had on jeans and sneakers and a western shirt, green-and-blue plaid with yokes that came down into points above the breast pockets.

The woman was up then, too, the older man moving across the room. The woman went to the man in the western shirt, said, "Daniel," almost in a whisper. She hugged him, and it took the younger man a few seconds to react, to move his hands from his sides, his face down to her hair.

The older man stopped a few feet away, his arms crossed, his hands holding his elbows. He had a new cigarette jammed between his index and middle finger. He looked at Daniel, then at the floor. He tapped his foot, then ran his hands up and down his arms as if the room had suddenly gone cold.

John turned back to the TV, tried to watch what was going on there. A sitcom was on now, one he usually watched with Lora each week. He recognized the faces of the people on the television, but he couldn't think of any names. Here came the star of the program, and the audience clapped. The star didn't have to say or do anything, just walk onto the set. He had to wait for the applause to die down before he could deliver his first line. He gave it then, and the audience broke up, everyone laughing.

But John was listening for the three behind him, back there in front of the double doors. He listened, but only the woman spoke. He heard the words "special people," heard "God" and "gone." The words seemed to float up into the room separate and distinct.

Then Daniel spoke. He said a couple of words, and then the name Mary came out, then he said "baby," both words taut and dry in his throat, and then John heard the man's breath quicken. He looked up from the TV—those people on the set now foreigners, people he'd never seen before speaking words he would never understand, though it was still the same sitcom—and saw that Daniel had leaned again into the woman, his face again in her hair.

The older man still stood a foot or so away, his arms still crossed, and John watched as he slowly reached a hand up to Daniel's shoulder, held it above him for a moment. The older man seemed to be watching his hand, wondering if he should let it touch this other man, and then he placed it on Daniel's shoulder, moved it back and forth and up to Daniel's neck and into his hair.

Daniel leaned his head toward the man's hand, rubbed his cheek against it. His eyes were closed.

John turned back to the set.

A few minutes later they were gone, the three of them back through the double doors. John hadn't looked at them again.

He watched the television, tried not to think. Gradually the faces there became familiar. This was a new program, another sitcom. He watched it, laughed a few times while he tried to stop thinking.

Halfway through the next program, a crime drama, he felt a tap on his shoulder. He jumped, turned to find Lora standing there at the end of the sofa.

John looked at her. One side of her face was lit by the colors from the TV, the other washed in the faint yellow from the lamp at the far wall.

She said, "What's wrong?" and bent down to touch his face.

He let out a breath, blinked. "You scared me," he said.

"Sorry," she said. He felt her hand against his face, his cheek rough with a day's growth. He wondered how she could touch him as gently as she did. She smiled, said, "Nothing's wrong. Gunderson told me to just take it easy, stay off my feet as much as I can. And to drink plenty of fluids. That was the main thing. To drink plenty of fluids to keep me floating."

"That's all? Nothing's wrong?"

"Nothing," she said. She straightened up, glanced at the set.

"Then let's get out of here," he said, and they left, stepped back through the double doors to the green tile corridor and the elevator, then back along the brown linoleum squares through the emergency ward. He kept his eyes down, quickly walked past the rooms where he'd seen all those people earlier.

They went to a Wendy's drive-thru on the way home, got burgers and fries and frosties because neither of them had eaten yet. John pulled back out onto the highway, and Lora spread out her napkin, draped it over her belly. She looked at him. "My bib," she said, and they both laughed.

He stopped at a stoplight, and she picked up her burger, leaned forward in her seat to take a bite. John looked at her there in the dark of the car, her skin gray, her red knit shirt and sweatpants and face all differing shades of gray, and he thought about telling her what he'd seen. He wanted to warn her, to tell her of things that could come, but there was nothing he knew to say.

Brothers

We were getting radio stations you wouldn't believe, as will happen on the desert at night. We were headed back from Phoenix in Tim's pickup, a Mrs. Conoley's rocker-recliner tied down in the bed, ropes run back and forth across that thing so tight that all you might see move back there were the stars above us if you looked out the rear window.

This was the stretch of road between Blythe and Indio, the first piece of California that seems like it might last a year before you make the hills and sand outside Palm Springs, then drop down into the low desert toward Indio, which is the date capital of the world. But that was still a good sixty miles ahead of us if it was a hundred yards.

Tim is my brother, though you might not be able to tell that by looking at us. He's taller than me and a couple of years younger. He is a quiet guy, but he will have his moments when he will say or do something, and you will laugh, count on it. We will be at a party or some such shindig our wives wanted us to go to, and just when things are looking the most dead he will walk up to me, his face all straight, and say, "Do you have a dollar?" "Sure," I'll say, and go for my billfold. "Good," he'll say, "I've got one too. Let's trade." Little jokes along this line.

He's heavier than me, too, and always has been. Just heavy enough that, say, if we were in a police lineup, you wouldn't think we were relations. His hair's a little lighter, too, and wavy, whereas mine is a dark brown and straight, which my wife says is actually limp.

But the radio stations. The night out there as dark as tar except for stars cutting out their own light made this the perfect night for picking up radio stations from all over, and I was flipping the radio dial back and forth across the numbers, listening here and there for things. If I tuned in some station in Arizona or California I just skipped over it, looking for exotic places, places I'd never been before. First there was Boise, and then had come Salt Lake City, and then some town in Oklahoma. Then, believe it or not, we started hearing music with a slide guitar and some guy singing out soft and sweet in a foreign tongue. It was beautiful music: the slide guitar slow and clear, someone else strumming a regular guitar, a quiet tom-tom sound, and then it clicked. This was Hawaiian music, like what you'll hear Don Ho do.

I turned to Tim. I said, "That's Hawaiian music. We're getting Hawaii."

Tim leaned forward over the steering wheel, turned his head toward the music. "That's right," he said, and eased back in the seat.

The DJ came on, said it was Hawaii. Hilo, he said, and the call letters, and I nodded to myself because I'd already figured it out on my own and here was my brother, who'd confirmed my suspicions. We were getting Hawaii out here between Blythe and Indio.

We were on our way back from a wedding we'd gone to in Phoenix. Some old high school friends of ours who'd been living together out there for eleven years had finally decided to get married. Tim and I thought we might see some of our buddies out there, but we were wrong. Who would drive all the way to Phoenix to see somebody get married? We two, in fact, were the only people other than Don and Diana we knew. We ended up leaving early to get the rocker-recliner. We were picking it up for a client of Tim's, a Mrs. Conoley, who, when she found Tim would be going to Phoenix over the weekend, offered him one hundred dollars to bring it back from her sister's.

He's a gardener, a good one, too, and can count among his clients several people who live up in Newport Hills in big squared-off houses. He makes good money at it, too, but you take one good look at his hands and you can see that that money didn't come easy: scars and callouses and beat, old red skin. He's got three Mexicans and one Vietnamese in under him now, so he's doing all right.

Me, I'm a newspaperman. Hah. I drive truck for the Orange County *Register*, dropping off bundles all over Orange County. You'll see me sometimes. I'm the big orange-and-white truck that stops somewhere in the middle of your tract every morning, throwing bundles onto some kid's driveway. That's me, flashers and all going. It's an all-right job, I guess. Not as much money as Tim, but we've got a little house. We're okay, Julie and me.

So we're in the desert listening to Hawaii. Modern world, I was thinking, this is the modern world we're living in, when we started losing the station. At first it was a little wave in the sound, a little grate, as if somebody'd been sprinkling Hawaiian beach sand over the DJ's microphone, and then the world and its shape took over, and we started moving out from under where those AM waves were landing back on Planet Earth. Static started in, shaking through the sweet music so that the sound was clear and gentle, then shoved into static, then back to clear. This moving back and forth was getting faster and faster until one second it was music, the next tinfoil.

I reached to the dial, started fiddling with it again, trying to home in on Hawaii, to keep that sound from the other side of the world here inside the cab of the truck. I leaned closer and closer to the dial, stared at the green numbers, trying to figure exactly which little line between 105 and 130 brought Hawaii here.

"Turn if off," Tim said. "Just turn the goddamned thing off."

He'd said it loud, I guess. Too loud for inside the cab. I couldn't see much of his face for the dark, but I knew he was ticked.

I clicked the thing off, slowly leaned back in my seat. I put one hand on my lap. With the other I took hold of the window knob, popped the window down a crack. I looked out my window. There was nothing but greasy brush out there, every few feet another bush and on and on, one after another for as far as you could see, all the way to the mountains out there, black as old engine oil, then the stars jutting out above them.

Tim had been chewing over something since we'd picked up the rocker-recliner. Maybe even before that. What I remember is that after we'd left the wedding we'd followed the directions Mrs. Conoley had given him, and ended up in some posh neighborhood off Central Avenue. We pulled up into the circular drive of a stone and mortar house, and climbed out.

Right then a fat old woman wearing too much makeup and not enough clothes—she had on a high-cut neon-orange one-piece—came rushing out the door and told us she didn't want the truck in the driveway, but on the alley. We'd had to climb back in, drive around to the back of the place where the rocker-recliner sat square in the middle of an empty three-car garage, oil spots in all three slots.

He pulled the truck up, turned off the engine. He reached under the seat and brought out a coil of rope, and we got out.

We stood there a few minutes, neither of us saying a thing, just waiting for that old woman with no sense of bodily pride to come out, tell us what was up. We didn't dare step into the garage. Tim will be the first one to tell you you never go onto someone's property without them knowing you're there, preferably watching you. He told me once about how he tripped a silent burglar alarm houses like this will have. He had leaned against a window while trying to get at some weeds under an oleander next to the house. A minute later there in the driveway and street were four cruisers parked at crazy angles, doors open, officers squatting with guns out and cocked. They'd made him surrender his hand-clippers there on the spot.

So we waited. We waited, and we waited some more. Maybe fifteen minutes altogether, the sun sliding down all this time toward the cottonwoods that lined the alley behind us. Finally Tim called out, "Hello?" He pushed himself off the fender of the truck, took a few steps toward the garage, then called out again. Nothing. He went that way the fifteen yards to the garage, calling out every few steps, then listening, until finally he made it to the chair. I was still hanging back, only a few feet from the truck.

He looked down at the chair. "Shit," he said, and leaned over, pulled a yellow slip of paper from the seat. He looked at it, slowly walked over to me, shaking his head. He handed me the piece of paper. It read:

Gardener:
This is the chair.
You must be careful with it.

It was written in big, girlish handwriting, the *i*'s dotted with big circles, the capital letters three times bigger than necessary.

I looked up at Tim. I said, "This is the chair. We must be careful with it." I laughed a little, but he didn't, just turned and headed into the garage, started muscling the chair by himself until I got there to help.

He started out gardening by mowing lawns afternoons when we were kids. Actually, the lawns he mowed had been my route, but after a couple of years of it I gave it over to him. Of course at that time I didn't know what he would do with it, didn't know he would end up making more money per year than me, that I would even end up mowing yards for *him* for money as I did one summer when I'd been laid off at the newspaper. But it makes me happy to be able to say I sponsored the guy back then, got him his start.

From then on out all he wanted were things that he could use for gardening: for Christmas one year he got a wheelbarrow, and one birthday he'd gotten a secondhand gas edger. For high school graduation he got a front-throw reel mower. I was happy all those years getting a BB gun for Christmas, or a balsawood airplane for a birthday, or new tires for my '63 Nova, which is what I got for my graduation. All those years I was just looking at my nutty brother and his gardening stuff, just wondering what went on inside that head of his.

Which is what I was thinking when, right after he'd jumped on me to turn off what little bits of Hawaii we could have had along with us, he turned to me and said, "I'm quitting being a gardener."

I turned to him. He'd already looked back out the windshield to the road and that broken white line.

I said, "You're just pissed at that woman. At letting us wait, ignoring us like we were toads or less."

Tim was still looking out the windshield. He said, "I'm not pissed. It's not that. I deal with that crap every day, people regarding you as if you were trash just because you do something to the ground and you do it with your hands. I've put up with that since day one." All I could see was his profile, black there in the cab, beyond him, out his window, greasy bushes, black mountains, those stars.

"Then what is it?" I asked, and I waited for an answer. I waited, but when after a couple of minutes he didn't say anything, I shrugged, leaned forward, started to reach for the radio. I was lonesome for Hawaii, for Boise, Boulder, anywhere, but when my hand touched the knob Tim said, "Don't." He'd almost whispered it this time.

I looked at him. He had turned to me, and I could see the

faintest face, the green light from the dashboard just filling in his cheeks, his chin, his forehead. His eyes were still gone, still in there somewhere. He looked back to the road.

He cleared his throat, scooted around in his seat. He said, "You know," and stopped. He took a breath. "You know," he started again, "Lew's wife died. Betty. Sunday morning."

Lew was my brother's next-door neighbor, an old guy, in his seventies. He was a big guy, six-two and thin, his white hair slicked back on the top and sides. I'd met him only once, when I'd been over at Tim's borrowing, of all things, a lawn mower. Lew had walked up the driveway, said to Tim, "Who's this bastard going to abscond with your professional materials?" We'd all laughed, and he gave me this smile. He had bad teeth on top and bottom, but he had the easiest smile, so simple you didn't even mind the teeth, the kind of smile that made you feel like you'd known him since you were a kid, like he knew the good and bad of you all at once.

I'd never met Betty, though. All I knew about her was that she'd had a stroke three or four years ago.

"Massive brain hemorrhage," Tim went on. "She'd been in the hospital three weeks when she died. The night she had the hemorrhage, the night she went into the hospital, everything came out to the house. It was three in the morning. Police, fire trucks, ambulance, the works came out for it. Beth and I watched the whole thing from the bedroom. We thought they'd had a fire or something."

He put both hands on the wheel. I could tell he wanted to talk, finally figured that this was what he'd been working on in his head the whole trip, and so I settled in.

"I was mowing the yard," he started up. "Sunday morning, about seven, when Lew pulls up. He sits there in his car a minute before the motor's off. I knew that she'd died. I could just tell. He didn't even have to get out of the car. I cut the mower right then.

"We used to mow our lawns together, I was thinking. Lew and

I used to get up every Sunday morning and do our lawns, match each other stroke for stroke up and back. We both had Bermuda in front, and we'd have contests to see who could cut his lawn closest without losing the green. That's what I was thinking about."

He stopped, looked out his side window a second. "Keep going," I said, though I knew he'd go ahead whether I said anything or not.

"Azaleas," he said. "The man had azaleas in the flower beds in the front yard, along the sidewalk, next to the mailbox. He had them in his backyard, too. Against the back fence. Bordering the patio. Azaleas."

I tried to picture azaleas, but couldn't get anything together. All I could remember of Lew's yard were green bushes.

"All colors," he said. "Violet, white, pink, red. Azaleas everywhere. You know why? It was because Betty loved them. When things blossomed, the whole yard went crazy. So much color. Pink and white and red. Azaleas."

I reached up to the visor, pulled out the pack of cigarettes he had wedged up there. The last ones we had were all the way back at Gila Bend, where we bought them at a Circle K. We figured we'd need the things in order to pass the time. Now here was the time.

I pulled out a cigarette, shook one out for Tim, and put the pack back above the visor. He pushed in the lighter.

We got the things lit, and I took in the first hard smoke. I knew I'd catch hell from Julie when I got home, as I've quit the nasty habit four times in recent memory. But smoking now was different, I would tell her. There is a distinct difference, I would say, between smoking in the desert and smoking while throwing bundles out the back of your truck. This smoking was okay, I would say.

Tim just pulled on his cigarette, didn't even inhale it. He shot out the smoke, then went on. "He had Bermuda there in the front," he said, "and Saint Augustine in the back, that stuff with the wider blades. The thick stuff you need to cut just as close as the Bermuda. And the trees he had over there were all things you could eat, I was thinking. In the front yard he had an olive tree, and around to the side yard was a plum tree. In the back he had dwarf lemon and orange trees, planted in those oak half-barrels. He had an avocado tree and a peach tree back there. And against the other side of the house he had a grape arbor. Just a trellis mounted six feet above ground, but Lew liked to call it his arbor. He told me it was Betty who wanted trees, trees that would grow things you could eat. That's why he planted everything."

We sat there a few minutes, quiet. I was having a good time with the cigarette, menthol air down in my lungs like some old friend.

"He used to bring her out into the sun while we worked on our yards," Tim said, and I could tell by his voice that he was smiling. He was happy. "He'd set up a lawn chair in the middle of his driveway, then walk her out and set her down in the sun, and then we'd go at it. She sat there without moving, you know, because of the stroke, and she watched us. Sometimes Beth would come out, too, maybe brush out her hair for her, or just sit next to her in one of our own lawn chairs, and talk to her, the four of us out there in the sun."

His voice cracked a little, and I took it to be the cigarette. Maybe he'd finally decided to inhale, I figured. He let out his smoke, took a deep breath.

"Some nights I'd lie awake and think about what it would be like," he said, now a little slower, a little quieter. "What it would be like to have just those things to worry about. Just your own yard, your own trees, your own azaleas. Nobody else's. Some nights I'd get up and look out the bedroom window at Lew's yard, and just wonder. I'd start envying him, even though he had a wife who'd had a stroke, who he had to take care of all the time." He stopped a second, readjusted himself in the seat. "He fed her," he said. "He washed her hair. He took her to the bathroom.

He taught her to walk again. Each day for seven months he made her get out of bed and take a step, one more step each day, until by the seventh month he'd gotten her to walk all the way to the kitchen."

We'd finished our cigarettes by now, and at almost the same time we both reached to stub the things out in the ashtray. Tim didn't notice that he'd almost burned a hole in the back of my hand, his eyes so fixed on the asphalt in front of us.

Tim had gotten me to thinking of Julie, though, and I tried to imagine for a few seconds doing all those things for her, taking care of her, but I couldn't come up with anything, no real pictures in my head of her leaning over the sink, me scrubbing her scalp, or of me taking her to the bathroom. I just couldn't muster those pictures.

I shook out another cigarette then, which of course would make it two in a row, which of course constitutes taking up smoking again, but I really didn't care. I just wanted Tim to keep talking. I put the pack in my front shirt pocket, popped in the lighter.

"That's tough," I said. "That's a tough life, for certain." It was, too, I figured. The lighter popped, and I took it out.

"So what I did was this," he said. "It'd been three weeks since Lew had touched his yard, not since Betty'd gone into the hospital. Lew had already gone into the house by that time, so I pushed the mower out onto the sidewalk and went over to his yard and went in on his lawn. It was all I could think to do. I went at it. I mowed his grass as close as I could, and then I mowed it again. I took out the edger and went all the way around the yard, turned the dirt in the flower beds, then swept everything off—the sidewalk, the porch, the driveway—and I hosed everything down. I could feel Lew watching me all this time, somewhere in the house, but it didn't matter. I was thinking about the lawn, about how it still didn't look right, something still didn't look good about it.

"I went around to the side gate and let myself in, wheeled the mower and edger in, then did the backyard. I gave it the same treatment as the front. I never cut grass any lower in my life. I swear it.

"All this time Lew's back there in the house, watching me, I can tell. I felt like he was right there with me, right behind me sometimes, watching me weed the beds, trim the yard, dump grass into barrels. Sometimes I'd look out the corner of my eye to the sliding glass window on the porch, but I never saw him. I just kept on."

He stopped talking, and I think we both saw the rabbit at the same time. It was just there all of a sudden, a skinny Western Jack, all back legs kicking out, black-tipped ears sticking straight up. It'd run out onto the highway, then made a crazy turn and started zigzagging up the road, as if it thought it had a chance of outrunning us. All this in a second, the time it takes you to sit up and take a cigarette out of your mouth, which is what I did.

Then it stopped, sat there like a cutout in a shooting gallery, the reflection of the headlights in its eyes, that ugly bright yellow.

Tim swerved to miss it, took us off the road onto the shoulder, both of us bouncing up and down in the cab, rocks and gravel shooting up into the fenders and sounding like fireworks. He swerved back onto the blacktop, and we were riding right along, no difference in anything, except Tim. He had both hands tight on the steering wheel, sat hunched up over it.

"Relax," I said, even though I was still feeling the rocks in my stomach, too. "Just relax. It was only a rabbit."

But Tim just sat there, whispered, "Son of a bitch," then went quiet.

Two cigarettes later we hit Desert Center, a poke-up of lights, an overpass, and then we were back on the desert.

I'd already smoked half the pack, and the guilt was starting to wear off. Cigarettes will do that to you when you start up again. The first couple of them will make you feel as guilty as all hell, like everyone you know or ever knew who'd smoked and'd quit or had never even started were watching you, but along about the tenth one down, halfway through that first pack, you start thinking, Hey, I deserve this. These cigarettes are okay. My reward. And then the eyes of everyone on you just start dropping away, fading out, until you're the only one, just you and a friendly cigarette there at your lips.

That was how I was feeling, Julie still a couple hundred miles away, probably getting ready for bed now in a little house in Garden Grove, where on good days you could catch a hint of the ocean in the air, the salt and the green of it.

I smiled at nothing, then turned to Tim. "Keep going," I said. "You're not done yet, are you?"

He didn't move.

I said, "You want another smoke?"

He nodded then, a quick jerk of his head, and I was there with a cigarette already pulled out for him, had the lighter pushed in before he got the cigarette settled between his fingers. When the lighter popped I pulled it out, and Tim leaned over. I put it to his cigarette, the orange glow lighting up his face, and I could see his eyes for the first time since the sky had gone dark. They were a little glassy, maybe a little wet. He pulled away, and I put the lighter to my own cigarette.

"Things," he said, and that was it for a minute. He just sat there, leaned his head to one side. "Things, things still didn't look good," he said, and now his voice was all low, almost whispering, and I tried to figure what was coming next. I thought that I could figure my brother out, thought I knew what he would do one minute to the next. Now his words were all quiet, his eyes full. He might as well have been crying.

"Things still didn't look good," he said again. "I figured a good trim and weeding would do the trick, but it didn't. So I went to my garage and got out the garden shears. That was it, I knew. Things had to be cut back. Things were shaggy. I started with the oleanders along the left fence in his backyard. Then I got a pair of pruning shears and cut back his rosebushes against the back fence. They didn't really need it, but I still cut the hell out of them. Each snip, each branch falling made me feel better.

"I finished that and started in on everything else in his backyard. I cut everything back. I knew he was watching me, but I didn't look to see if I could catch him. I got a pair of lopping shears from my garage, and cut back his avocado tree, his peach and plum trees. I cut back branches until it looked like dead winter and some big storm had torn leaves, branches, everything off. I went to the grape arbor and cut the hell out of everything. Everything will come back, I was thinking. It'll all come back. And then I went at the azaleas. I got down on my knees and started trimming and shaping and trimming some more. That was when Lew finally came out."

He took a swipe across his eyes with his forearm, his cigarette waving through the air in the cab. He'd only taken one drag, and I knew the ash must have been an inch long if it hadn't fallen into his lap yet. If it had, he hadn't made a move, hadn't noticed a thing. His eyes were on the road, both hands back on the wheel.

He took a deep breath. "I looked up from the flower bed," he said, "and there he was with his arms crossed, his head lowered. He didn't look at me, only at the bushes. He nodded, and I went on. I didn't say anything.

"He went around the yard then. He went to the arbor and touched the branches, went to the orange tree and put his hand around the trunk. He squatted down and ran his hand across the grass, that grass I'd cut so short. Then he came over and watched me finish shaping the azaleas. Then I led him into the front yard and started working on the azaleas there. We never said a word. There was nothing to say. He just watched me." He stopped again, took another breath. "Then I came home. I went into the kitchen to the sink and started running the water so I could wash my hands, and when I looked out the window over the sink, there was Lew, standing out in the middle of the street. He'd gone into the house and brought out a camera. It was an old thing, ancient. But there he was. He had the thing up to his face, and he was taking a picture of the house, of the yard. He was taking a picture."

He leaned forward, stubbed out the cigarette he'd taken only one drag from.

That was it. He'd finished his story. He put his right hand on the wheel, moved his left hand to his forehead, his elbow against the window.

I waited a few seconds. "That's sad," I said. I turned to him. "That's sad about his wife." I finished off my cigarette, then let three more telephone poles pass us before I said, "If you're really quitting gardening, then I'll take your route over. I'll take it off your hands." I was serious, too. I said, "I'll take dirt on my hands over newsprint any day." I laughed a little, then coughed, felt the smoke down there, already settling in my lungs.

He turned and looked at me. He didn't say anything, just looked at me.

I said, "Hell, it makes sense, doesn't it? I gave the damned thing over to you when we were kids in the first place, if you'll remember. It was me who gave you my business. Who else would you give it to? I'm your brother, remember?" I was smiling at him.

He turned back to the road. Then he slowly shook his head. He rolled down his window all the way, his arm pumping the handle around and around as fast as he could.

The wind from outside shot into the cab, warm wind from off the desert. You wouldn't think the air would be that warm, everything so dark out there, but it was. Tim put his elbow out the window, that piece of him sticking out into the dark.

"Too much cigarette smoke," he said above the roar of the wind. "Too goddamned much cigarette smoke," he said. He was still shaking his head.

I put my hand up to my shirt pocket, felt for the pack. I pulled it out, put my finger into the top of it. There were only two cigarettes left. Only two.

"You're right," I said, more to myself than to anybody else. I coughed, and there was that smoke again. "You're right," I said so he could hear me. I took the pack, shoved it up above the visor, up there where it belonged.

I reached for the radio, turned it on. I wheeled the knob back and forth ten times before I turned the thing off. Hawaii was long gone. There was nothing. Not even a station from Indio or Blythe or Desert Center, if they had one. Only static all the way across.

I sat back, looked at Tim, my brother, saw his profile, his wavy hair jumping around in the wind. I tried to figure him out. I tried to figure what he would do next.

He had to be hungry, I knew that. The last thing we'd had to eat was a sliver of wedding cake two hundred miles and a rocker-recliner behind us. I knew he was hungry, and I imagined us dropping down into Indio, down into air even warmer than this, the low spread of lights below us that would be Palm Springs. We would pull into a Denny's, go in and take stools at the counter, wait for an overtanned waitress to come up to us, ask us what we'd like. And I'd look at her, thin wrinkles beside her eyes and under her chin from all that sun, and I'd look at my brother, the same one sitting here with me in this cab, and, just to lighten things up a bit, I'd say to the waitress, Would you guess we were brothers? Look at us. Would you guess that? I might even lean over toward him, put my arm around his shoulder, give a grin like what kids will do in photo booths. We're brothers, I'd say. Believe it?

What Our Life Is Like

Their washer broke down some three weeks after the warranty went out.

"This is what our life is like," Millie shouted from the basement that night. Steven was upstairs in the den, shaping the hull of the model ship he was working on, the *Benjamin Latham.* Millie's voice came to him more through the heating ducts than through open doors and along hallways.

He went downstairs to the kitchen, opened the basement door. He was three or four steps down when he saw water.

Millie stood next to the washer in her tennis shoes, the water just below her ankles. Her head was in the washer—it was a top loader—and then she stood straight, leaned her head back. She yelled, "Steven!" her eyes closed. She drew his name out loud and long.

She stopped, looked at the ceiling. She was waiting, he imagined, for some sounds, some movement on his part.

"I'm right here," he said. He was sitting on the fourth step down.

She flinched at his voice, then smiled a second to try to make him think he hadn't scared her.

"Why is it," she started, "our life is like this? The warranty goes, the washer goes. Our life is worse than those commercials where everything goes wrong." She started using her hands, one fist clenched and shaking away at cobwebs, the other hand on her hip, knuckles white, red nails digging in. She wore her hair short, cut just above the ears and a little off the collar in the back. Steven thought she liked it this way because when she yelled like this she could shake her hair and make it shiver just so; it wouldn't swing around and hit her in the face like a little girl's would. That hair just sat close on her head and trembled.

"Our life is like this," she shouted, her hair helping her. "A basement of water, a broken-down washer, filthy clothes."

He said, "Calm down. I imagine one of the boys can fix it. I can call and have one of them come over on Saturday."

"Saturday isn't good enough. Saturday won't do."

"Saturday it is, then," he said. He went upstairs.

A few minutes later Millie shouted up at him, "I'm going over to the Laundromat. It's eleven-thirty at night. It's an all-night place over at Kingsgate Plaza. I may be mugged, I may be raped. What do you care? You just want clean clothes. That's what our life is like, too."

He said, "Be careful."

She slammed the door. He heard the car start in the garage.

He kept shaping the hull, most of the grit worn off the sand-paper. Each time he ran his hand along the wood it seemed only a few grains of wood fell. Then he heard the kitchen door close, thought that maybe she had forgotten something. Change, maybe.

He glanced at the clock on the shelf above his worktable. It was 2:07. She had been gone two and a half hours. Still, 2:07 was not late in their household. He went back to work.

Millie pushed open the den door.

"Guess who I just met?" she said.

He said, "I can't."

"A dancer. A dancer. Can you believe it?" She came into the room, pulled an extra stool from inside the closet over to the worktable. She put the stool next to him, then sat down, her hands clasped between her knees.

"I can believe it," he said.

"A dancer," she said. She leaned over the table, made like she was interested in things. "Anna is her name. That's a beautiful name."

"Beautiful," he said, still sanding.

"She is beautiful. We sat and talked and talked and talked. She was interesting to talk to. A little flighty. Artists, you know."

Steven turned the hull over in his hand, and over again, just holding it there, feeling the wood.

"She's a graduate student over in the Theater and Dance department at the university. She's five-ten, almost too tall, you know, for a dancer, and wears her hair back in a bun. She's from Oneonta. She kicked her leg up until her nose pressed her shin, right there in the Laundromat. She's incredibly lithe."

The word "lithe" came out as if it had two syllables, and he thought how odd that word sounded coming from her. It was a word he had never heard her use before. He turned to her then, hull in hand, and wondered if it was a word Anna had given her.

The washer went unfixed. Millie didn't seem to mind, though, and went to the Laundromat around midnight a couple of nights a week, her trips eating up every bit of change that entered their house.

Then one night she came home with their clean clothes and the news that Anna was coming over for dinner.

"She's blue," Millie said. "She's got nobody around here she knows." They were up in the den. Steven was working on the same boat, now piecing out the deck. Millie had a cup of coffee and was leaning against the worktable. She put the cup to her lips, took a sip. The coffee cup had the call letters of the local public radio station painted around it. Not long after she met

Anna she started listening to this station. They had a fund-raiser one weekend, and she had called in, pledged twenty-five dollars. That was how she got the cup.

Steven said, "Why isn't she home? In . . ."

"Oneonta. There's lots of infighting going on up there with her family." She put the cup to her lips again.

Infighting. This was another of those words, he knew.

Steven answered the door.

"Good evening, Mr. Kelloran," Anna said.

Millie had not told him anything about her eyes. They were green, and as sharp and glistening as polished stones. In the moment he opened the door, her eyes looked through him and back to the kitchen, through the boys' empty rooms, down into the basement, up to the bedroom and into the den.

"Oh," he said. "Oh." He opened the door wide, shuffled his feet back a few steps, and made a gesture with his free hand to usher her in. He thought he was smiling. He felt older.

She was wearing a gray flannel cape with big wooden buttons, and had it off and over her arm before he got the door closed. Under the cape she wore a black turtleneck sweater, a black wool skirt, black tights and black suede half-boots. Around her waist was a paisley silk scarf, knotted at the hip. Her face, white against her black clothes, looked pale, almost brittle.

"Allow me," he said, and reached for her cape. His voice had sounded stiff and slow to him.

Millie came in from the kitchen. She held her hands out in front of her, and Anna took them. They gave each other the smallest hug, their shoulders just touching, then kissed each other's cheek.

Millie took a step back from Anna, said, "You're looking elegant this evening." They were holding each other's hands, looking at each other's clothes.

"And you," Anna said, smiling.

Steven looked at Millie. She was wearing an ivory silk blouse, silver embroidery around the cuffs and down the front. He had bought it for her years ago, back when the boys were still living at home. She had not worn it since then. And she had on a pleated gray skirt, gray stockings, and black pumps. Anna was right. Elegant was the word.

Millie and Anna turned to him. He was wearing a flannel shirt and an old pair of khaki trousers, a couple of resin spots here and there that seemed bigger now than when he had put the pants on.

"Steven," Millie said, "this is my friend and compatriot Anna Jensen. Anna, this is my husband and sometimes friend Steven."

The three laughed at this, and Steven shook her hand. Her hands were whiter than her face. Her nails were bitten to the quick.

"How do you do?" he said, and felt a wash of heat across his face that might have been a blush.

The first chance he had, he went back to the bedroom and put on a sweater, a nice pullover cable knit. Millie finished making dinner while Anna set the table with crystal and china from the cabinet. Steven got the silver from underneath the bathroom sink.

For dinner Millie brought out Raspberry Chicken, a dish Steven had never seen around the house before. Along with it she had prepared wild rice and broccoli with orange. Once everything was on the table, Millie came out of the kitchen with what looked to Steven like a twelve-dollar bottle of champagne. She handed him the bottle and a white dish towel.

He held the bottle in his hand a moment. He looked up at Millie. She turned, moved her fork an inch or so.

"Champagne," Anna said.

Millie said, "Of course." She motioned for them to sit down.

Steven read the label again, then popped open the bottle, poured all the way around. What the heck, he figured. He picked up his glass, raised it in a toast.

He held the glass in the air for a few seconds. He said, "To these two elegant women." It was all he could think to say, but they both smiled. They touched glasses, took sips of the champagne.

Anna and Millie talked during most of dinner. Neither ate much. They talked about dancing, mostly, both of them dropping what seemed to Steven might be big names if he knew anything at all about dancing. Millie kept right up with Anna, too; Anna would mention a couple of names, then Millie would match her with two of her own. They both sat there, plates barely picked at, fingers of both hands laced around their champagne glasses, elbows on the table.

Steven cleared the table. He expected Millie to say something to stop him; instead, when they saw what he was doing, Anna and Millie moved from the dining room to the living room.

Steven went back to the kitchen, saw pots and pans everywhere. An empty carton of cream sat on the counter next to a few thawed raspberries in a puddle of red juice, and a half-grated orange. He made room for the dirty dishes on the counter, pushed some utensils aside.

There, under a saucepan lid, he found a cookbook. He picked it up. It had a clear plastic jacket around it, numbers on the spine. Millie had checked it out of the library.

He thought about this a few moments, then put the book down, opened to the page Millie had left it on. He put the lid back over it, then finished stacking plates.

He went into the living room. Millie was sitting on his recliner, leaning back in it, her legs crossed at the ankles. She held her glass with two fingers, the other arm on the armrest.

Anna was on the sofa and sat leaning forward, one leg over the other, her foot in the black suede half-boot rocking away to some rhythm. Champagne washed around in her glass.

He walked between them and toward the end of the sofa. He said, "Excuse me," as if he were a guest in his own home, but he didn't mind. It was pleasant, in fact, putting on airs in their old house. Anna and Millie talked around him as he passed.

He sat at the far end of the sofa, ran his hand across the crocheted doily straight-pinned into the arm. He looked around the room. There was this sofa, the beige drapes, the television and television stand, a rocking chair with a seat that needed reupholstering. There was the celery-green hi-lo shag carpeting, and the chocolate-brown recliner.

He turned to Anna. She and Millie were talking about health and fitness. Anna said that she had an aerobic exercise program she had designed herself. She went through it every morning before she drank her cup of hot water and lemon. Millie said she was going to sign up for Jazzercise at the mall.

Steven said, "So Millie tells me you're very lithe."

The two of them looked over at him. Millie blinked.

Anna, her face silhouetted by the lamp at the end of the sofa, turned to Millie, then back to Steven. Though he couldn't see her face, he knew those eyes were working again, taking him and everything around him, even the old cluttered room, right into her.

"Well," she said, "a dancer has to be. It's part of her life. His or her life. There are plenty of male dancers out there, too." She gave a small laugh, and Millie joined her.

He said, "So give us an example. Show us something lithe."

Millie sat up in the recliner, reached across and touched Anna's knee. Anna turned to her.

Millie said, "He's talking about the first time I met you. When you, you know, did your kick right there in the Laundromat." She laughed, glanced at Steven. "Remember?"

"God," Anna said, "that was so long ago." She put a hand on her forehead, her fingers stiff and straight against the skin. "I'd forgotten about that."

"Well, why don't you do something for us?" Steven said. "Why don't you go ahead and show us something here?"

"Yes," Millie said. Steven looked at her. She was smiling. She touched Anna's knee again. "Do," she said.

Anna put her other hand to her face, held it over her eyes. She stood, then slapped her arms to her sides. She shrugged, stepped around the coffee table. Steven could see her face now. She was smiling, too.

She said, "If you insist," and went to the middle of the room.

Steven stood, leaned over to move the coffee table. "Do you need this out of the way?" he said, and started moving it.

"No, no," she said. "Don't bother. It's not in the way."

He moved it a foot or so closer to the sofa and sat down.

"Here goes," she said. Slowly she brought her leg out to her side, her arms straight down in front of her, fingers locked, palms down. She kicked high, her leg swinging out above her waist at her side. Steven looked at her face, waited for some grimace, some show of strain, but none came. She just smiled and smiled, her leg moving gracefully beneath a black wool skirt that billowed out in an arc at her side.

She stopped. She shrugged again, her face a little flushed. Here was the strain, Steven thought, but she grinned, put her hand over her mouth, and he knew it was only a blush.

She started to sit down, but then turned to him, put a hand on his arm. "Do you have a stereo? A radio?" she said. Her face was lost to him again in the light from the lamp behind her.

"Certainly," he said. He got up, went across the room to the television stand. He opened the cabinet beneath the set, switched on the hi-fi they had in there. It was tuned to the public radio station, but Steven switched it around to an easy-listening station. A soft rumba was playing.

"A rumba," Anna said, and she was out in the middle of the room again, just barely moving her feet, her arms bent at the elbows and out in front of her. She was dancing the rumba. She said, "Come on, Millie, let's dance." She started for Steven, moving her arms out in front of her, pointing at him. "Steven," she said, "do you know how to rumba?"

Millie stood, then was doing a little dance, too. "He sure does," she said. She was laughing, looking down at her own feet, surprised, Steven thought, she could still dance.

"No," Steven said. He put his hands on his hips, shook his head. "No, no. It's been too long."

"Steven," Millie said. She looked up. "You know you know how."

"No," he said. "You two dance. You two go ahead."

Anna turned, saw Millie dancing. "Oh, Millie," she said, "that's wonderful." She took Millie's hands, and the two of them went at it.

Steven let them dance like that for only a minute or so, though, before he joined in. Anna and Millie laughed, and he did, too.

The next number was a waltz, and Millie and Anna sighed. They both wanted to dance it with Steven, but he chose Millie. They started dancing, moving around the room, his hand on her back, her fingers in his palm. Occasionally he would turn and see Anna standing next to the recliner, swaying back and forth, her hands behind her back. After a couple of minutes she came over and tapped Millie's shoulder. She said, "May I?"

Millie smiled, curtsied, and then Steven was dancing with Anna. He had expected dancing to be something different with her, but it was not. Her back felt the same as Millie's, her hand in his the same. She was taller and put more into her movement, dipped a little lower, swayed a little more. But if he had closed his eyes, he could have been dancing with his wife.

Later Steven put on an old polka album, and they took turns whirling around the room, nearly knocking over furniture. After that he turned the radio back on, switched stations around and found an old rock-'n'-roll station. They did the Twist and the Stroll.

They danced a few more numbers, and then Anna said she had to go.

Steven helped her on with her cape. Millie gave her another kiss on the cheek. Steven opened the door for her, and he and Millie followed her out onto the porch. Anna thanked them again. Even out there in the light cast from inside, Steven could see her eyes were green.

When she was at the end of the walk, she turned. "See you at the Laundromat," she called.

Steven turned to Millie. He could see her face, the puzzled look. Then Millie said, "The Laundromat. That's right."

Anna waved.

Later Steven and Millie lay awake in bed. They had been lying there an hour or so. Dishes were still stacked up in the kitchen. Food was still out. A library book sat face down under a saucepan lid.

Steven said, "You forgot about the Laundromat, didn't you?"

He waited a few seconds, and then she moved her arm up over her head, rested it there on the pillow. He counted off thirty seconds more, waiting for her answer, then sat up, put his feet on the floor.

"I can't sleep," he said. He stood, pulled on his robe. He still had the rest of the deck to build for the *Benjamin Latham*, then the mastwork, after that all the rigging. "I'll be in the den," he said, and started for the hall.

"Steven," Millie said.

He turned. "What?"

She said nothing. He put his hands in his robe pockets.

He said, "Library books, model ships. Dancing. It's not so bad."

She rolled over toward him. He looked at the bed, at the floor. He took his hands out of his pockets, put them at his side. He sat on the edge of the bed.

There was more to say, he knew. He waited for her to start. He smoothed his hand over the sheets, brushed away invisible dust.

Christmas Presents

Paul pulled into the shopping center parking lot, his son David seated next to him. Today was the last Saturday before Christmas, and the lot was jammed with cars. Even worse, snow had started the night before, obliterating the painted lines on the asphalt, and beneath the snow lay a thin sheet of ice left by the rain two days before. For a moment Paul thought of dropping David off at the entrance to the drugstore, letting him wait there until his father found a spot. But then he had visions of David walking across the ice, slipping and falling and breaking a bone, and he decided to keep the boy with him.

When he finally parked the car, they were at least one hundred yards from the door. He turned off the engine, looked at David. He felt scared somehow.

Later that day Paul would be going to the hospital to bring Kate and their new baby home, and the fear he felt just then made his heart sink: they had talked a lot of the baby coming, offered to let David place his hands on Kate, speak to the swelling there any number of times. But each time their son had backed away from them, tried hard to leave the room for his own bedroom no matter how soothing their words, how gentle their touch.

David wanted nothing to do with what Paul could only guess was something his son could not yet understand, the look on David's face as he backed away showing some fear of his own, his forehead wrinkled, mouth closed tight.

There was no way to know how he would react once the baby was home. Jill still did not exist for David, Paul knew, the boy's sister only a baby somewhere, his mother gone for a couple of days. They could only bring Jill home and hope to live their lives as a family, Paul and Kate doing their best to give as much care and attention and love to both their children as they could.

"Let me carry you," Paul said, and then climbed out of the car. He pushed the door shut, felt the snow on his face as he came around to David's side.

David had already climbed out and closed his door. "Watch," he said, and put the bottom edges of his parka together, slowly started zipping it up. When he got to the collar, he tucked his chin down, finished zipping until he reached the top edge, his mouth and nose now hidden inside the collar.

"I did it myself," David said, "so you can't carry me."

Once inside, David unzipped the parka by himself, too, and Paul pulled off his gloves, brushed snow from David's shoulders. Strings of red and green and gold tinsel hung everywhere inside the store, strains of "White Christmas" in the air, plastic Christmas trees with blinking lights and too many ornaments perched atop the end of each aisle.

David stood inside the door a moment, taking everything in.

"Now we're here to get your mother a Christmas present, remember?" Paul said. "Earrings and bracelet. That's what you decided. And we have to get a present for Jill, too."

David nodded, then ran to a bin of red-mesh candy-filled stockings just past the row of checkstands. He picked one up, held it close to his face.

Paul followed him, picked up one of the stockings himself. Inside it were a few flat pieces of chocolate wrapped in gold foil to look like coins, a foil-wrapped chocolate Christmas tree, a small book entitled *Santa Meets Frosty,* two green and two red suckers.

David said, "We can get one of these for Mommy," his eyes still on the stocking.

"For Mommy?" Paul said. "What about the earrings and bracelet?" He put the stocking back on the heap.

"Oh," David said, looking up at him. "Yeah," and then his expression changed, his face puzzled, one eye squinted nearly shut, one corner of his mouth up. "We have to get a present for Jill?"

Paul nodded. "Your sister."

David only looked back at the stocking.

Three-thirty the Thursday morning before, Kate's first contractions had come. The baby was twelve days overdue already, so that when he squeezed open his eyes to the light from the lamp on the nightstand, it was with some relief he saw her sitting up, her pillow wedged beneath the small of her back, her shoulders pressed against the headboard.

After an hour and a half of timing, of standing up and walking around and climbing back into bed and taking measured, logical breaths the childbirth instructor had called *avenues to deal with the advent of birth,* Kate had finally said, "Let's go."

Paul was dressed by then and pulled the already packed suitcase from beneath the bed. He carried it downstairs, then went out the kitchen door and across the backyard to Jim and Nancy's.

Outside, the air was almost warm for December, a light rain having fallen sometime in the night, and his tennis shoes were wet by the time he made it to their back door. He tapped the windowpane, knew that Nancy would be up and waiting for her policeman husband to come home from his regular shift.

Nancy pulled back the curtains inside the door window, smiled at him. She opened the door, and said, "Look." She pointed at her feet.

Paul looked down. Beneath the hem of her robe were the

scuffed and muddy tips of her workboots. He looked up at her, felt his hands in his pockets, but couldn't remember having put them there.

She said, "I knew it was going to be tonight. I knew it when I sat down to watch TV last night, that tonight would be the night," and then she was pulling the door closed behind her, and walking off toward a house, *his* house, he realized as he turned to follow her, a house with lights on in a bedroom upstairs and in the kitchen below.

Nancy said, "I've already left Jim a note I'm over here. When David gets up, I'll make him waffles and bacon. I knew this was the morning." They were at his door, and she pushed it open, moved inside to their kitchen, where Kate stood, the suitcase next to her, a hand on the small of her back. She and Nancy hugged. "Go," Nancy said. "Have your second child. Now."

"One last thing," Paul said, and he left the kitchen, went upstairs to David's room.

The boy lay sleeping, but Paul prodded him, whispered his name until David rolled over and sat up. He scratched his head.

"David, we're going to the hospital now," he whispered, one hand just touching the boy's shoulder. "Mommy's going to have the baby now. Mrs. Thompson is here to take care of you, until Daddy comes home later. Okay?"

David's eyes were still closed, but he reached up to Paul, whispered, "Don't go, Daddy," his face in a frown, Paul could see from the light in the hall. "Don't go," he whispered again, but Paul only held him a few extra moments, then let him fall back to the bed, pulled the comforter up to his chin. Paul kissed him, then turned, headed toward the door. Once there, he looked back at his son one more time, felt himself try to smile. David was already asleep.

Eight hours and two small doses of pitocin later, a girl had been born.

"What's her name?" asked the doctor on call, a woman they had not met before but for whom he suddenly felt certain love for having given them this child. She handed him the baby, and it seemed weightless in his arms.

"Jill Elizabeth," he had said, and as he held his daughter, still warm from inside her mother, the baby's skin still slick and bloodied, he realized he was the first in her life to call out her name.

He brought the baby to Kate, who had by this time begun to shiver with the loss of blood and fluid, but through her quivering she smiled. "Jill Elizabeth," she had managed to get out, the smile on her face wavering, her uplifted arms shaking. Paul laid Jill on Kate's chest, placed a hand on the baby's back to make sure she wouldn't fall.

And it wasn't until then, his wife and new child before him, the room filled with the sounds of his daughter's crying, that he thought of his son back at home, pictured him at a breakfast of waffles and bacon. Paul wondered if David would even remember his father coming to him in the early morning, kissing him good-bye.

"Let me see those again," Paul said once they were in the driveway back home. He hadn't yet turned off the engine, the wipers going, defroster on high.

David brought from inside the large paper sack on his lap the two small gold cardboard boxes. He let the bag slip down his legs to the floorboard, and carefully placed a box on each thigh. He reached for the left one, opened it up. Inside was a bracelet, a thin gold chain almost lost in the cotton lining the box. David held it up, smiling.

Paul looked at it, nodded and made the okay sign, just as he had when he'd let David pick out the jewelry from the rack at the drugstore cosmetics counter. "Now the earrings," he said, and David lost the smile, put the lid back on the box, placed it on his left thigh, picked up the one on the right.

Inside the box were two thick gold rings the size of silver dollars; in the center of each ring floated a shiny blue star. They were big and heavy earrings, nothing Kate would ever wear, but again Paul gave him the okay sign, nodded. David smiled up at him.

David said, "Mommy will love these," and brought them close to his face, his eyes open wide. With one finger he touched each star, the touch brief, tentative. Then he held the box with both hands again.

Paul said, "They're beautiful."

They had been in the house no more than a minute, just inside the door and working off their boots, when Paul heard the knock at the kitchen door. "That's Mrs. Thompson," he said to David, who, oblivious, sat on the floor, both hands struggling with a boot.

Paul went through the living room and past the darkened Christmas tree, presents from relatives and friends already stacked beneath it, and into the kitchen. He opened the door, and there stood Nancy wearing sweatpants and a pea coat, snow edged up the sides and nearly over the toes of her workboots.

She came into the kitchen, a few stray snowflakes floating in behind her, and Paul noticed for the first time the darkening afternoon sky, already upon them. He felt his stomach start to twist, and stood looking out the door a few moments, Nancy behind him, stomping her feet.

"Close the door," Nancy said. "You don't want the house frozen up before your baby comes home, do you?"

Paul started to close the door, but paused a moment longer just before he pushed it shut, surprised somehow at the dark gray slice of sky between door and jamb. He thought of Kate, of Jill, of this being his daughter's first day home, and suddenly the house seemed quiet to him, more quiet than he could ever remember it being, the only sounds those of Nancy taking off her coat, and the whisper across his backyard of snow falling on snow.

He pushed the door to, and David ran into the kitchen, both boots off, the paper bag in his hands. "Look what I got for my mommy," he yelled, and dropped to his knees, slid a foot or so as though the kitchen floor were ice. He put the bag on the floor, pulled out the two gold boxes, said, "This is what I got for Mommy," and placed them on the floor in front of him. He took off the lids, admired the jewelry only a moment, long enough for Nancy to say, "How marvelous," and squat next to him, place her hand on his head. Then he put the lids back on, pulled from inside the bag the two red-mesh stockings Paul had let him buy.

"And these are presents for me," he said. He held one out to Nancy, who took it in her hand. She glanced up at Paul, said, "These are wonderful," her mouth in a big grin. She looked back at David, gave him the stocking, and stood.

Paul said, "One's for you, and the other is for Jill, remember?"

David didn't move, and Paul felt again the uncertain fear of what his son would do once his sister was home. He looked at Nancy.

Her eyes were on David. She shrugged. "It's about that time, isn't it?" she said, and now she looked at him, smiling, as though nothing were wrong, David ready and eager for the daughter Paul would be bringing home soon. "Two-thirty is when you have to be there, right?"

"That's right," Paul said, and he could feel his stomach going now, the feeling at once joy at Jill coming home, a new baby, a *girl*; and regret for the lost time with his first child, five years that seemed suddenly gone before him.

He stooped next to his son. "I have to go to the hospital now," he said, searching out David's eyes, trying to get his attention. "I have to go get your mother and your sister now. I wanted to help you wrap Mommy's present, but maybe we can do that when we get back. But right now I have to get to the hospital. Okay?"

Finally David's eyes met Paul's. Paul said, "I love you," and put his arms around his son, held him.

David said nothing, and when Paul pulled away, David's eyes were on the stocking, his hands holding it tight.

• • •

Kate was standing next to the bed, a loose-fitting dress on. The suitcase lay across the bed, and she was leaning over it, zipping it closed.

"Hey," Paul said before she saw him, "you're not pregnant anymore."

She turned to him, gave a weak smile. She put her hands to her stomach, pressed the material of the dress to her skin.

"Now it begins," she said. "The long road back."

Paul kissed her, then picked up the suitcase, placed it on the floor beneath the window. He put his hands on his hips, said, "So where's the girl?"

Just then a nurse wheeled a Plexiglas crib through the doorway, stopped at the foot of the bed, and the room fell away from around him.

In the crib lay their daughter, wrapped tight in white blankets, her pink face and sprigs of brown hair the only color in all that white. She was asleep, her eyes closed, the lids a pale blue, her mouth pursed.

He stood at the crib, heard Kate say, "Here she is. Our Christmas present all set to go home."

"That's right," the nurse said, and reached into the crib, brought up the baby in her arms.

But the nurse's movements seemed too quick and mechanical, and Paul reached out, said, "Let me hold her."

Kate, arms already up to receive the baby, took Jill from the nurse. She looked at Paul, gave a small smile. "First let me put on her outfit," she said, and placed her on the bed. On the bedspread lay a pink outfit, the color so pale he hadn't noticed it before. It was a bodysuit, snaps down the front and down the inside of either leg. At the waist was a little rim of lace, a sort of tutu, and he remembered the outfit, given by Nancy at the shower she had put on for Kate. Paul watched as Kate peeled back what seemed layer upon layer of blanket to reveal his daughter in a white sack-like gown, hospital issue. Kate slipped the gown up and over Jill's head, and the baby stirred, seemed ready to awaken.

Paul took in a breath, ready for the baby to cry, but nothing happened; Kate only took off the baby's diaper, her hands moving quickly, practiced.

She looked up at him, the diaper in her hand. "It's wet," she said, and smiled, looked at Jill, then at Paul again. She said, "You put the next one on. I want you to get back in the swing of things."

Paul shrugged, stood next to Kate. From nowhere the nurse produced a diaper and a wipe, held them out to him. "You're on," she said, and smiled, her head tilted to one side.

He turned to Jill. There lay his daughter, naked. He knew how to change diapers, had done it often enough with David. But now this was his daughter, and suddenly he forgot everything: how to hold a baby, the tone of voice he should use, if he could walk and carry her at the same time.

He took the diaper and wipe, felt the breath he had taken in a moment ago leaving him, and then he did what he figured was the only thing he could do: he cleaned his daughter as best he could. Then the nurse handed him a miniature powder container, and he dusted Jill, slipped the diaper beneath her, peeled back one adhesive strip and then the other, and cinched the diaper around his daughter's waist.

He brushed the powder from his hands on his pants legs and smiled down at his daughter. Kate came to him and kissed him, moved past him to the bed, and began putting the outfit on Jill. The nurse said, "Job well done."

A few moments later Jill was dressed, wrapped in blankets again, nowhere a trace of the pink outfit she had on. Still she slept, and Kate took her up. "Now you can," she said, and passed to him their daughter. He took her into his arms, and the helpless surprise came back to him, the truth that he knew nothing about how to care for her.

He looked down at his daughter's face. Her lips quivered a moment, then relaxed, her eyelids the same pale blue.

He looked up at his wife, the nurse. They were smiling, waiting for him, and he felt his feet begin to move, his body coming around the foot of the bed. In his arms was their daughter, and suddenly she was no longer weightless, no longer only blankets. "Jill Elizabeth," he said to Kate. "Jill Elizabeth," he said again, this time to himself, and in those words was some power that enabled him to smile, head out of the room and into the yellow corridor.

The sky was near-black when Paul turned onto their street, the road recently snowplowed, gray snow heaped over sidewalks. In the backseat were his daughter and his wife, and so the trip that had taken them fifteen minutes Wednesday morning, the streets new and clean and glistening from the warm rain, had today taken an hour. Neither had spoken the entire trip home, the car silent except for the hollow rush of the heater, the wet hiss of tires on the road.

Their Christmas lights were on, the house ringed in red and blue and orange and green. The garage door was already open, the light on inside. "The Christmas lights," Kate said. "That's nice Nancy turned them on."

"Yes," he said. He turned into the driveway and glanced in the rearview mirror, saw the dark silhouette of his wife behind him. Though he knew there was no answer, he said, "What do you think David will do?"

Kate was quiet as he edged into the garage, then said, "I don't know." She paused. "We'll see."

Before the engine was off, the door from the kitchen flew open, and here came David, his hands behind his back. "Mommy, Mommy," he shouted, and ran around to the passenger side, stopped at the door where his mother usually sat. Then he saw her in the backseat, smiled wide.

Kate opened her door, and David moved back to her, leaned in and kissed her.

"My boy," Kate said, and hugged him. "Do you know how much I missed you?"

David only smiled, shook his head in answer. He said, "Guess what's in my hands."

Nancy was already at the window behind Paul, peering in at Jill. "She's beautiful," she whispered. Paul opened his door, climbed out. He stood next to Nancy, looked through the glass at his daughter. Her eyes were open now, one fist next to her face. She looked smaller than ever, cradled in the big car seat.

Paul looked over at Kate, next to the car seat. She had already guessed which hand, and was unwrapping one of her Christmas presents, David standing next to her, a hand still behind his back. He was turning back and forth, smiling with all his teeth.

The wrapping job was mainly Scotch tape, Paul could see, the bow merely knotted ribbon. Kate finally got the green-and-red-striped paper off and opened the box, held up the gold bracelet. "It's absolutely beautiful," she said, turning it one way and another. She slipped it on her wrist, held it out to David for him to see.

"Yep," David said.

Paul came around the back of the car to their side, saw the second box in the hand still behind David's back. He squatted next to David, whispered in his ear, "Those are Christmas presents. Are you sure you don't want to wait until Christmas to give the other one to Mommy?"

David quickly turned to him, still smiling. He said, "Isn't this Christmas?" and handed Kate the second box, this one done up with even more tape.

Paul looked at Kate. "These are the Christmas presents he bought you today," he said. "I guess we're opening them a little early."

Kate reached the hand with the bracelet out to him, touched his arm. "That's fine," she said, and smiled.

She started in on the second box, and while she carefully tore at the paper, she said to David, "Do you know who's sitting next to me?" She turned and nodded at the car seat.

David lost his smile, stood on his toes to see past his mother. "What's that?" he said.

"Your sister," Kate said. "Jill Elizabeth."

Paul said, "Your baby sister."

David turned and slowly started around the back of the car. Paul stood, followed him.

Nancy opened the door for David just as he rounded the rear of the car, and he stood next to the car seat. Paul put his hands on David's shoulders.

David slowly leaned over her, his hands at his sides. Kate had a hand on the edge of the car seat. Paul could see the bracelet on her wrist.

Paul said, "Well, what do you think?"

David stood straight, pointed at the baby, his hand a tight fist except for the index finger.

He said, "That's my sister?"

Paul said, "That's right," and gave his son's shoulders a small squeeze.

But David twisted free from Paul, scrambled between the open car door and Nancy, ran in the door to the kitchen. Nancy looked up at him, her arms crossed in the cold, then turned to the kitchen door.

This was the moment Paul had feared would come. He had wondered how his son would do it, how he would begin to accommodate his life to this intruder, his sister, and now here it was: their daughter home, their son hiding somewhere in the house.

Paul stooped, looked across the car seat to Kate. She said nothing, only sat with the half-opened second box on her lap, one hand still on the edge of the car seat.

Paul said, "I better go find him."

But just as he stood, here came David again, running through the door from the kitchen and around Nancy to the open car door.

The stockings were in his hands now, and before Paul could

say or do anything, David had placed one of the stockings inside the car seat, said, "This one is for you, and this one is for me."

David looked up at his father. "Okay?" he said.

Paul could only smile, put his arms around his son's waist, hold him tight. "Okay," he whispered.

Kate reached in and touched the stocking, ran her fingers across the mesh. "You went all out," she said.

David nodded, said, "Now you finish opening your present," and Kate turned back to the box, continued peeling back tape.

Paul watched her eyes once the lid was away. He had figured she might laugh, or sound too condescending, praise the gaudy earrings too much, but she simply took an earring in each hand, held them up before her. She smiled, shook them a moment so that the blue stars floating in the center shimmered with whatever small light there was in the garage. She turned to David, her mouth open to speak.

But David was leaning over the car seat, and from where Paul was he could see David touch a finger to Jill's small fist. Then David leaned even closer, and Paul saw his son's lips touch his daughter's cheek.

He looked at Kate, knew she had seen the small touch, the kiss. He could see her eyes glistening, her lips together. She was looking at Paul, and slowly, carefully, she took first one earring, then the other, and clipped them on.

Work

When we make love, I forget we live in a one-room apartment above a liquor store four blocks from the ocean, and that our bed folds up into the wall. I forget I work part-time at the liquor store, Linda at the Golden Sails Inn on up Pacific Coast Highway. She's a cocktail waitress and wears a short, tight dress cut low across her breasts, layers of ruffles beneath her skirt so that it sticks out like a tutu.

I forget that each workday, before she leaves and I go to work downstairs, I zip up her dress for her and say, "You're a fool, going to work in a getup like that."

She says, "Who's the fool? Me? Or you, working part-time in a liquor store?"

We always say those things before we go to work, but I am kidding. She makes most of our money. I also forget that she has stopped smiling when she says, "Me? Or you?"

I work. I do a lot of the odd jobs around the store. I sweep the sidewalks, sort returned bottles, wash all the windows whenever Dick, the manager, tells me to.

About a week ago I asked Dick if I could go full-time at the liquor store.

"Daryl," he said, "first thing is, is that we're not a 'liquor store.' 'Liquor store' makes it sound like all we do is sell Muscatel, NightTrain, and T-Bird. We're a specialty store."

Dick calls it that because in the rear of the store, behind the coldboxes, is a section of dirty magazines, some greeting cards, a poster section and display rack. Still, he didn't answer my question. I didn't ask again.

A guy in a wheelchair came into the store tonight. He was about thirty-five, brown hair down to his shoulders. He wore an Army fatigue jacket, the name Jenkins stenciled above the right breast pocket. He seemed to have no problem opening the front door and wheeling in.

"Howdy," I said from behind the counter.

"How you doing tonight?" he answered.

I said, "Oh, all right, I guess."

I watched him wheel around the store, looking at booze, chips, magazines. He spent some time flipping through the poster display rack, and when he finally came to the register he had one of the posters and an Almond Joy.

"I wish you had a couple more of this one," he said. "I know some people'd like this one. Are those back there all you have?"

"Yes," I said, "but let me go back and check. What number is it?"

He handed me the rolled-up poster. I read the numbers out loud from off the yellow tape on the end of the roll, then went back to the display rack and checked all the cubbyholes for his number. There weren't any more.

Then I went through the display rack, just to see which one he'd picked. I wondered if it was the nude blonde running on the beach, or maybe the brunette with her hair covering only the least bit of her breasts. I knew those posters by heart.

Then I found it. The poster was an autumn scene of oak and maple trees lining a clear stream. In the distance a log-pole bridge crossed the stream, a bridge it would have been difficult to cross even for me.

I walked back to the register, shook my head without looking at him.

"Didn't think so," he said, and gave me the money.

He was at the door before I said anything to him. I called out, "Sure you don't need any help?" I started to move out from behind the counter.

"No, no," he said, waving me away. "If I don't make it a practice to move myself, I'll lose it." He opened the door. "So long," he said.

I said, "Thanks."

At midnight I closed the store. I usually go upstairs and watch TV until Linda comes home a little after one and undresses in front of me, not always because of me, but because of the one room. But tonight I decided to drive up PCH to the Golden Sails for a drink before she got off. I parked the car and went into the lounge, sat down at the bar and ordered a beer.

"Where's Linda?" I asked the bartender. He smiled and pointed to a table where five or six businessmen laughed and smoked, ties loosened, collars unbuttoned.

Linda was serving drinks all the way around. The men laughed as she set down cocktail napkins and then drinks. Linda leaned across the table and served a man who pulled the swizzle stick from his drink and put it down the top of her dress, wedging the stick between her breasts. The men laughed. So did Linda. She pulled the stick out and dropped it back into his drink while the man she stood next to placed his hand on her skirt, pressing down the ruffles until his hand contoured her buttocks. She served the man his drink last, then traced his lips with her fingertip.

She turned from the table, headed back to the bar, but stopped smiling when she saw me there. I heard her call my name once as I pushed the doors open and went for the car.

She came home a little after one and shook a fistful of cash in my face. She said, "See? This is it. This is it. You think I like this? I do it for the money. So we can live."

I yelled, and then she yelled some more. I unzipped her dress for her, and she undressed in front of me, peeling off the top of her dress and wriggling out of the ruffles. Then we made love.

I forgot about the night, about my job, about Linda. The only thing I remembered was that guy in the wheelchair at the door, pushing it open, wheeling out into the dark, and I knew I'd be a fool if I didn't take his advice and move myself away from here.

But then things came back: first Linda, then the darkened room, cars on the highway outside, and the world moved right back in. I started over again, the way I do each time.

Rum Cake

On my way home from work I stopped at the video store next to the Alpha Beta, and rented a VCR, a couple of tapes. It was something I'd never done before, renting a VCR. There would be no one around when I got home, and I figured that was the best way I knew to pass time until my wife, Pam, and my two boys got back. The three of them are up in Portland at Pam's aunt's funeral, and due to the economics involved, I opted to stay home: kids over two fly full fare now, and since our first boy, Marty, is four years old, we had to pop three hundred and two dollars. My other boy, Larry, is just over two, but we lied to the ticket agent, told her he was twenty-one months, and she believed it. Larry's a little small for his age, which is something we sometimes worry over, but in this case it was a sort of blessing.

In addition to the lack of money, I didn't go because I get along with her mother even worse than Pam does. It's the sort of thing you see in comic strips and on TV, where the son-in-law gets along so poorly with the mother that they can't stand even to talk on the phone to each other. "Count me out," I said to Pam the night we got the call from her mother, asking for the four of us to head on up there. "It'll cost too much money, for one thing," I said, and then I didn't go on to name the other thing: the idea of being cramped up in Aunt Joan's house with my mother-in-law.

Pam only nodded, made the phone call to the travel agent, told about how, because of the kids, she would need bulkhead seating.

The tapes I got were kind of strange. I don't know what got into me. Maybe it was this heat. Phoenix is no picnic in July. I got *Doctor Zhivago,* a movie I hadn't ever seen before, and *White Christmas,* which I've seen a dozen times, and which kills me at the end when all these guys show up for the reunion with their old general, while outside it snows. I figured if *Doctor Zhivago* got too boring I could always blink it off, stick in *White Christmas,* and then fall asleep in front of the set with all that snow falling in Vermont at the end.

The lady at the counter, a short black woman wearing a red smock over her street clothes, helped me fill out the papers she needed in order to rent me the VCR. Then she started showing me how to work the thing.

"Is your TV cable-ready?" she asked, holding a black wire in either hand between the tips of her index fingers and thumbs, as if they were hot, ready to spark.

Our TV *was* cable-ready, though when we bought the thing a year ago that didn't matter; all we wanted was a color TV, tired after six years of having that old black-and-white set we'd gotten at the swap meet just before we got married.

"It is," I said. "It's cable-ready," and I got this look on my face like I knew exactly what she meant, though I knew diddley about the holes behind the set. We still had an aerial on the roof. We couldn't afford cable.

"Good," she said, and just dropped the wires, a smile on her face as she wrapped the cord around the long black box. She put my two tapes in a white plastic bag, set them on top of the VCR.

I pushed in the door, the VCR about to flip out of my arms, and the bag with the tapes in it fell on the floor. Then the phone rang, and I had to make my way to the sofa, put the VCR down, turn and close the door behind me. An open door in this heat is like burning dollar bills, and if it was an important call, I figured whoever it was would call me back.

But still the phone rang, and when I finally picked up the receiver, Pam said, "My mother. Save me from my mother."

She was whispering, and in the background I could hear people talking, voices up and down, and plates and glasses, and I could hear, too, the boys, Marty hollering, Larry crying.

I said, "Come on. It can't be that bad."

She whispered, "It is," and said, "Mom, take Larry. He won't settle down." Then I heard her mother make this clicking sound with her mouth, a sound a chipmunk might make. A sound that drove me crazy, because not only was it annoying, but it meant she thought you weren't much of a person for whatever reason, in this particular case Pam for not being able to quiet down Larry.

Her clicking sound came across the wires, clear from Portland, and already I was tensing up. I said, "Okay, I believe you. But I can't save you. You have to make it through on your own." I paused. "And you don't have to stay there for three days. Like we said, if you want, you come home as soon as you can." I paused again, then said, "But you know about those SuperSaver fares. About having to stay over until Sunday. You know."

I heard her do something at the other end, maybe pull a door closed or shut herself up in a closet, because those voices and plates and glasses and the sounds from the boys all seemed to die down.

She said, "We'll stay. Most likely, anyway. It's not that bad. It's just that when my mother gets going with guests in the house—you know how she is."

I nodded. "Yes," I said. "I know. Please don't go into it."

"Thanks tons," she said, "for wanting to hear from me."

"It's not that," I said. "I want to hear you. Just not about her."

"Fine," she said, and paused. "You're not going to believe what happened, how Aunt Joan died," and I imagined Pam in whatever room she was in, say, the hall closet, surrounded by old and musty coats, people milling around just outside the door, her mother swirling around them, making sure to keep the carpet clean, the coffee table free of sweat rings. She was talking to me in that dark of boots and umbrellas, her finger twirled up in the cord like she does, maybe her eyes closed, her brown hair down to her shoulders.

Aunt Joan was Pam's favorite aunt, not for the platinum and diamond cocktail ring she had promised Pam years ago, but for the good woman she was: a widow from the age of twenty-five, her husband killed in Italy in World War II when the jeep he was driving for a two-star general hit a land mine and flipped. Ever since she was able to walk, Pam had been dropped off by her mother to stay for weeks at a time with Aunt Joan, Pam's mother having been divorced when Pam was two, a divorce her mother didn't want, a divorce that ended up with Pam's father bringing into court a woman who'd sat in the witness box and said, "Yes, I slept with him. Yes, we committed adultery." That kind of divorce.

Pam has stories of how she and Aunt Joan would stay at the Timberline Lodge up at Mount Hood, and of camping together in some range of mountains an hour or so away, and of fishing in ice-cold streams for trout. Two women doing all these things, all things I never did. Things I look at my wife now and envy her for.

"She died," Pam said, "while she was making her rum cake."

"What?" I said, and I opened my eyes. I hadn't even known they were closed.

I looked around. The front room was dark, the shades and

curtains closed to help save the cool air in here. The place stayed this dark from April to October.

"You know," she said. "Baking her rum cake. Her famous rum cake?"

"Yes," I said, "yes," and I was back in her Aunt Joan's kitchen the one time I'd been there, only two months before Marty was born, Pam and I having figured we'd better get some traveling done before D-Day, when we wouldn't have the chance until who knew when to do things like drive the twenty-two hours it took to get us up to Portland from Phoenix.

It was about five-thirty in the evening, I remember, and we were sitting in her aunt's kitchen, Pam and I just having awakened from sleeping all day. We'd gotten in to her place about eight that morning after driving all day and night, and the two of us woke up to the sweet, sweet smell of her rum cake going in the oven. Blinking, yawning, we made our way into the kitchen, and took our seats at a table pushed against one wall, a little pinewood napkin and salt-and-pepper holder in the middle of a yellow-and-white checkered tablecloth. We were in the kitchen of a woman who'd never remarried, who'd never had any children, except, for all intents and purposes, Pam, and I can remember sitting in there, the smell of her cake around us, the light disappearing, and that hunger in me, the hunger of driving twenty-two hours and sleeping for ten with my wife curled up next to me, inside her our baby.

Aunt Joan came in. She was tall and thin and had beautiful, beautiful thick black hair, no gray at all, though by then she was in her early seventies. She smiled at the two of us, her hands in front of her and holding the bottom edge of her apron. She wiped her hands, and without a word, as if by speaking she might break the spell of a quiet kitchen, she opened the oven door, brought from it a bundt pan, placed it upside down on a plate in the middle of the table. She tapped the pan twice and gently lifted it to reveal her masterpiece: a cake, golden and warm, steam lifting up from it, catching bits of the late afternoon sun coming in through the jalousie windows next to the kitchen table. She stood over the cake, held the pan with two ragged potholders, and the three of us just sat there a moment. Pam and I smiled, taking in the aroma. Aunt Joan was smiling, too, but it was a different smile, something that went past pride, I think; something more like what real joy must be like, having your closest niece here with you, that niece whose diapers you used to change, the niece who maybe made you wish all the harder that you had gotten pregnant before your husband was shipped out only to get killed in WWII so that the young woman here with her husband would have been your own daughter. For some reason, I thought I could see this in her face, though she was only smiling down at a cake in the middle of the table.

We ate. I had three pieces before any of us even made any mention of dinner. After dinner I had two more pieces. As I remember it, Pam ate three or four pieces, too, but Aunt Joan hadn't eaten any. She'd only watched us, a smile on her face.

Marty's voice too loud behind my wife, Larry still crying, I was suddenly sorry I wasn't there in Aunt Joan's home, and sorry it wasn't me holding Larry. I wanted to take my pinkie and tickle him around the back of his neck. I'm the only one who knows that trick to settle him down, and I started doing some quick figuring: how long it would take me to get up there, how much farther back that three hundred dollars would set us. What I might have to do to get along with her mother.

"She was baking her rum cake," Pam said in a normal voice now, "when she died. She had the oven door open to look in at it, and her doctor figures that with her bending over like that, maybe her blood pressure just shot up or something, enough to—" She paused. She grabbed a hard, quick breath and said, "Enough to let her, you know, to—"

"I know," I said. "It's all right. It's—"

"And then her next-door neighbor, Minnie, came over," Pam

went on, that catch in her throat now nearly gone. "Minnie was knocking at the door, and knocking, and then she just opened it and came on in. And there she was. There she was on the kitchen floor."

Pam started laughing. At first I thought that maybe she'd really crashed and'd given herself over to sobbing there on the phone, but as I listened to the high, tight crack of sound deep in her throat, the near squeal that came after she'd gone silent a moment, I realized she was laughing. She said, "You wouldn't believe Minnie, what Minnie said." She laughed a little more, and I could feel myself trying to smile. "Minnie came in, and the first thing she did was take the cake out of the oven. And it was done. The top was a little light on the side that faced the open oven door, but other than that it was fine. 'It was instinctual,' Minnie said when she told me the story."

I heard the door swing open, and here came the voices, the glasses and plates, the general whirl of a house in crowded mourning. Larry was still crying, and I could hear Marty holler, "Thundercats, ho!" I pictured him with his silver plastic Thundercats sword, terrorizing all Aunt Joan's friends, and though I couldn't remember if you could see it or not from her house, I pictured outside the window Mount Hood rising, way off, snow up there. Cold, white snow.

Then came Pam's mother's voice a couple of feet away from the phone. "You're laughing?" she said. "You're laughing at a time like this? Well, then you take little Larry here off my hands and *you* tend to him, if you're going to close yourself up in here and laugh."

I heard the shuffle and shift of the baby from one set of arms to the other, heard Larry tussle and cry, but then he stopped, and he laughed. That was when I smiled.

Pam took a deep breath, and I knew she was smiling, too. She said, "So, got to go. Things are popping here." She paused. "I'm glad you were home."

"Me too," I said. "I love you."

"I love you, too."

I said, "Kiss the boys."

After I hung up the phone, I took a good look around the place: breakfast dishes still on the table, the water in the fishbowl cloudy and ready to be changed, last night's newspaper spread around my recliner. This, of course, all shrouded in the dark of the closed drapes, the only sound in here the airy hum of the air conditioner.

I looked at the VCR lying crazy on its side on the couch, those two tapes halfway out of the bag on the floor, and I remembered how I'd planned to fill in all this dead time.

It wasn't as hard to do as I'd thought it would be, though I was fifteen minutes fiddling with the set before I decided to break out the owner's manual we kept in the bottom junk drawer in the kitchen.

Then I popped in the first tape, *Doctor Zhivago*, and watched the opening shot: the movie begins with the camera lying face up in a grave, shovelsful of dirt one after the other heaved on top of it. All you see are faces looking down at the casket, mourning faces hard as iron that disappear with each new spadeful of dirt, the only sound the sudden thud of hard dirt on the coffin.

I didn't watch more than a few seconds before I was up from the couch and across the living room and punching the eject button. I didn't even bother rewinding what little I'd run of it, just got the tape out of the machine and back into its clear plastic box.

Of course the only thing I could think of was Aunt Joan and the fact she was going to be buried tomorrow. Buried, just like that, Oregon soil dumped on her coffin while somewhere sat a rum cake.

For a moment I thought of what it might be like for Pam if I were to die right now, what she would do with the two boys, and then I wondered what *I* would do if she were to die and leave me with the boys, and then I wondered what would happen if, say, their flight home crashed somewhere and all three of them were dead. I wondered what I would do, if I would quit my job and sell this house, or just go to work and back the next day, try to act like nothing had changed.

This is what I was thinking on a Friday evening in an empty house, Saturday and Sunday before me like two huge gray stones rolled into my living room. Static snow filled the TV screen, the sound filling the room, and I punched the mute button on the remote control in my hand, though I stood right next to the TV. I didn't want any more sound. I wanted quiet, or as much as I could get of it, for just a few seconds while I squeezed out of my brain the idea of my family dead in a plane crash somewhere outside of Flagstaff. I could see where these thoughts were going, where they might lead: only to me stupid-drunk on the couch the whole weekend, the TV on from one end of it to the other, while the drapes stayed closed and the air conditioner stayed on and my head kept itself filled with images I didn't want or need. I closed my eyes, blinked off the TV altogether, and headed for the kitchen.

I made a fried egg and bacon sandwich, left the pan right there on the stove; around the burner like some sort of oily halo was the spattered grease from the bacon, and my first instinct was to clean it up before I did anything else. But I left it there. I knew I would be cleaning it up eventually.

I couldn't imagine sitting down to the table for dinner, the empty cereal bowls at Larry and Marty and Pam's places, and so, the sandwich in one hand, a beer in the other, I went to the back window, the sliding glass door onto the little slab of concrete that makes realtors want to call these sorts of places Garden Town Homes. There are no gardens anywhere in our tract, no plant life to speak of except for the greasy bushes and the occasional lone saguaro some Landscape Architect set up. Other than that, what I looked out at, once I'd pulled the drapes back far enough so that I could see, was more gravel, a grapestake fence five feet high, and the beige asphalt shingle roofs of more Garden Town Homes.

But between the two houses behind mine I could see purple mountains, the short range that poked up from the flat desert floor as if they were somebody's afterthought. Mountains I could never remember the name of, small mountains, but with peaks no less sharp and jagged for it. From where I stood I could see just the small snatch of rock some ten or fifteen miles to the east, but what I could see gave me air, let me breathe some. There were mountains here, too. No Mount Hood, but mountains all the same, some wild ground not yet given up to all these cheap homes. I took a breath, felt hungry again, and I started in on the sandwich, the egg still hot, the bacon salty and crisp, the bread soft and warm. I ate, and watched those mountains, above them the seven o'clock summer evening sky, sky the blue of deep water.

After the sandwich I went back to the TV. I still had *White Christmas* to watch, the joy in seeing Danny Kaye and Bing Crosby and Rosemary Clooney and Vera-Ellen sing good songs: "Sisters" and "Counting My Blessings" and "Snow." And there were the dance numbers: "Choreography" and "Mandy," another one in which Vera-Ellen wears yellow shoes and a yellow short skirt and blouse, and dances with her partner in a dress rehearsal that couldn't be better than the real performance. I had all that to look forward to, and so I pushed in the tape, settled myself once again against the throw pillows, and watched first the FBI warning, then the Paramount logo, then *White Christmas* in big white letters against a red velvet background, on the borders little twists of green holly and red berries.

Finally the movie started: first a New England winter scene, the camera pulling back to show it's a painted backdrop on the front lines during WWII, and here come Bing and Danny doing a softshoe for the boys, the two of them in their Army uniforms. The camera cuts to an Army jeep pulling up, General Waverly—played by Dean Jagger—and the new general, his replacement, in the back. General Waverly tries to cover for his men, who, the new general maintains, shouldn't be celebrating Christmas Eve this close to the front. Waverly then instructs the driver of the jeep to use the shortcut to take this new general back to headquarters.

The driver pauses a moment, then says, "Yes, sir," and drives away.

But from the moment the jeep arrived on the scene, my eyes were on the driver. My eyes were on him, all clean-shaven, his eyes straight ahead, his jaw set, hands on the wheel at ten and two. He was a driver of a general's jeep, and as the two of them took off through gutted and shelled-out buildings to whatever "shortcut" it was this driver knew, I couldn't help but think of Aunt Joan again, and of her husband, and of his getting killed over there in Italy, driving a general's jeep. I knew this was only Hollywood, was only Irving Berlin and Danny Kaye and Bing Crosby and a Hollywood extra, "Yes, sir" his one line in the whole film, but I couldn't help but feel clear sadness for the driver, and I thought once again of that rum cake, wondered when it was Aunt Joan learned the recipe, wondered if her husband had even had the chance to taste the wonderful cake before he was killed, or if she had picked up the recipe after the war, when her days were filled with whatever emptiness goes along with the death of a spouse, in order to give someone else joy, shift the focus from her own grief to pleasing another loved one through the gift of that cake.

I watched the screen as now Waverly squatted in the back of the crowd of boys, listening while Crosby sang "White Christmas" to a windup music box, his thumbs hooked over the top of his coat belt, his blue eyes sad and wide open, the blue there nearly crystal clear.

I stood, went right to the sliding glass window, put my hands to the glass, and I could feel the heat from outside, turning the window into one huge plate of fire, my hands, cool from being inside, now nearly too hot to stand, but I did not move them. I held them there.

Between the houses were those mountains. They hadn't

moved, though I knew they wouldn't have. Still, the aunt I hardly knew lying in a coffin just waiting to be buried, my wife and two children up in Portland the night before her funeral, I needed to know those peaks were there, needed to know that something here wouldn't change.

But as I stood at the window, behind me and across the living room "White Christmas" over now and General Waverly chewing everybody out for how sloppy they looked, the mountains did change. The sun was nearly down now, and the peaks shifted from purple to gold to orange to red, all in what felt like a minute, beyond the peaks the still-blue sky, cobalt, ready for stars to break through any moment.

I turned, looked at the living room, now nearly dark, and I knew then that my wife would be different, too, when she came home, and that my children would be changed; they would be older, seem bigger, maybe more talkative, maybe even louder than before, after my spending three days alone in here, the only company a TV and a kitchen that needed cleaning up.

I saw it didn't matter who you were, whether you were a woman who knew how to bake a rum cake and who never imagined her husband might actually die driving a general around the Italian countryside, or if you were a lonely, scared husband and father waiting for his family to make it safely home, to walk in that door and drop bags and demand food and water and love; it didn't matter who you were because everything changed.

Now Bing and Danny and the entire company were singing to the general that they would follow him wherever he wanted to go, the picture from the set all the more colorful for the darkness, and so I went around the room, turning lights on: first the lamp stand next to the wall unit, next the ginger jar on top of the end table, next the kitchen lights, then the lights in our rooms, then in the bathroom. Everywhere were the signs of life I needed to see while the world went on, changed around me whether I wanted it to or not: blue sandals, almost too small now for Larry, lying in the hallway; three Matchbox cars and a bottle of purple shampoo on the edge of the tub; a blouse, a pair of Levi's and a cloth belt over Pam's end of the footboard.

By the time I made it back to the living room, Bing and Danny were at a club down in Florida watching Rosemary Clooney and Vera-Ellen sing "Sisters." For a moment I thought of stopping the tape, running it back so that I could see scenes I'd missed: that wall falling and nearly clobbering Bing, their names spread all over the front page of *Variety*, the two of them arguing about love and marriage and raising a family. I thought of that, of running it back to see all those things, especially the part about love and marriage and kids, but then I turned, sat down on the couch.

The house was lit now, and I could see everything around me. I lay back down on the couch then, my eyes on the set, and I smiled, hoping Pam had had at least one small bite of Aunt Joan's last cake, and that maybe, if they were lucky, the boys had gotten a taste of it, too. And I prayed that somehow, through some miraculous turn of events, some blessing way out of my hands, a piece might be left over for Pam to bring home to me.

What About My Lawn?

Barbara had seen it all from the kitchen window, had watched the car jump the curb, the rear tires throw grass and dirt across her front lawn, the brick mailbox stand crumble, the car stop. The car looked familiar, but Barbara could not place it. She walked quickly through the house and out the front door. She was still in her robe and pajamas.

She came down the porch steps and looked in the driver's side window at a woman bowed over the steering wheel. "Damn, damn, damn," the woman said. Barbara tried to open the door. It was locked.

She tapped at the window. "Excuse me. Excuse me, miss. Are you all right?"

The woman slowly looked up from the steering wheel. Barbara knew her.

"Janet? Janet Cummings? Janet, open this door."

Janet rolled down the window. Barbara saw an empty fifth of Scotch on the front seat. "God, I'm sorry, Barbara," Janet said. "Barbara, I have to talk to you. Oh, Barbara." She turned back to the steering wheel and sobbed.

"Janet," Barbara said, "come on inside. I can talk to you." She looked both ways down the street at the row of tract homes. "I'll talk to you. Just come inside." In one move Barbara reached through the open window, pulled the keys from the ignition, and opened the door. Janet fell out onto the grass.

Barbara looked at the tire tracks in the yard, at the torn sod in the finely manicured lawn. Janet lay face down in the grass, crying. Barbara dropped the keys in her robe pocket and hoped one of the neighbors had called the police.

She took down two coffee cups from the cupboard and filled them. "How do you like your coffee, Janet?" she said. She glanced at the clock above the range, wondered how long before the police would arrive.

Janet had stopped crying and was sitting at the dining room table. "Oh, God, Barbara. I really don't want any coffee. But black, just black." She sniffed.

Barbara set the cups on the table. "Janet," she started, as though nothing had happened, "it's been years. You still live two blocks over, right?" She sat down and forced a smile. "I can't remember the last time I saw you." She thought of the mailbox in the yard, the lawn torn up and the car still parked there.

"That's why I have to talk to you," Janet said. She put her elbows on the table, her face in her hands. "God, Barbara," she said, "you've got such a perfect family. The whole time we used to play pinochle, the whole damned time we used to play pinochle I always thought of what a perfect family you had."

"Pinochle! That's right," Barbara said. "We used to play. But, God, that was such a long time ago. Drink some coffee. You'll feel better." She straightened her robe over her knees, then sipped her coffee. "Hey," she went on, "and my family isn't perfect. Far from it." She laughed without looking at Janet. "You know what? Jack has taken to mowing the lawn at night. I mean, for twelve years he's been mowing the lawn on Sunday mornings, and now, all of a sudden, for the last five months he's been mowing the lawn at night. Can you believe it? He's rigged up a flashlight on the mower so he can see better."

Barbara was quiet a moment, waiting for Janet's reaction. None came. She continued. "And my oldest boy, William. He married a pretty girl named Elaine about two years ago. They moved to Arizona about six months back and haven't called in a month. That's a far cry from perfect."

"Shit," Janet said. Barbara flinched, almost spilling her coffee. "Shit, that's not anything. You remember my youngest, my Jackie? She went away to college for a year and came back married. Married, just like that." She tried to snap her fingers, but could not. "They got a divorce last month, too, just like that. Jackie moved back in, and her ex has slept over three times so far this week. And George has never mowed the lawn once, day or night. That's what I have to put up with. Shit." She twisted her napkin to a point and dabbed the corners of her eyes.

Barbara stood up. "Excuse me," she said, "but I have to go to the little girl's room." She smiled. She went upstairs to the master bedroom and called the police.

"So you still have a perfect family, goddamn you," Janet said.

"It isn't perfect," Barbara said. She sat back down at the table and looked at her nails. "Look at my youngest boy. My Kenny ended up dropping out of high school. Disciplinary problems. So not everything is perfect."

"What do you mean, 'Disciplinary problems'?" Janet said.

"Well, I don't think it's any of your—" she started, but then stopped. She crossed her arms. "Disciplinary, you know. All his aptitude tests said he was extremely bright. The school psychologist said he was just bored with school, so he just naturally got into trouble." She paused. "Not bad trouble. It seems he made some sort of explosive in his chemistry class. His teacher tried to throw it out the window and lost a finger. His pinkie. So I guess it was just a mutual agreement all the way around. He wasn't kicked out. He's in the Navy now. He's somewhere in the South Pacific at this very moment."

"Big deal," Janet said quietly. She stared at Barbara. "You've still got a perfect family. You think a boy in the Navy is bad? My oldest daughter, my Marilyn, ended up marrying a jerk who works the concession stands at Anaheim Stadium. He sells peanuts. He sells peanuts, goddammit." She slouched in her chair. "A boy in the Navy. That's a good one. My son-in-law sells peanuts, and you think the Navy is bad."

"He's only a machinist's mate," Barbara said. "Hardly what his father wanted him to do. Jack offered him a job as a merchandiser, said he could even have his own company car. But Kenny would rather work down in 'the bowels of the ship,' as he calls it." Barbara gave a quick laugh.

"So what?" Janet said. "So what? He's learning a trade, isn't he? My goddamn son-in-law sells peanuts. He makes peanuts selling peanuts." She laughed at her own joke. "Perfect family."

"To tell you the truth," Barbara said, neither wanting nor meaning to, "he's in trouble. Kenny is." She looked out the sliding glass window off the dining room to the backyard and the pool, the patio furniture, the rosebushes. She wondered when the police would come. She wondered why she had started telling Janet of her son's troubles.

"I heard from his commander yesterday," she said. "They caught Kenny smuggling marijuana inside his scuba tanks after they pulled out of Yokohama. His scuba tanks were filled with marijuana. He told them when he was going ashore that he was having them refilled."

She turned from the window and stood up. "There," she said, her hands on her hips. "That's your perfect family. Are you happy?"

She went into the kitchen.

Janet staggered after her. Barbara was already at the sink rinsing breakfast dishes.

"Do you have something to eat?" Janet said. "Some toast? Or maybe some cookies. I could use some cookies."

Barbara stopped rinsing. She stood still a moment and saw through the window the car out in the yard. She turned and smiled. She said, "I'm afraid I'm not being a very good hostess. Let's see." She crossed the kitchen to the counter and opened a teddy bear cookie jar, the bear's head the lid. "I've got some Oreos and some Vienna Fingers." She looked back at Janet. "You can have both, if you like."

Janet waved a finger at Barbara. "She married this peanut salesman because he got her pregnant. Right in my front room, on the floor. Marilyn told me all this on her wedding day, just before I was supposed to go down and sit in the first pew. She stood there in her wedding gown and told me she thought I would be happy knowing I was going to be a grandmother. I cried and cried, and all the time she thought it was because I was happy." She moved toward Barbara, who stood holding the cookie jar lid. "And now I have a grandson I can't see but once a week because I smoke and Marilyn doesn't want cigarette smoke around her baby." She stopped only a few inches from Barbara's face.

Barbara tightened her smile until she felt each tooth showing. "You know what?" she said quietly, almost in a whisper. She slammed the cookie jar lid back on. "My daughter-in-law Elaine, the pretty little girl my William married, got pregnant. William was the father. They'd been married a year. They both had good incomes. And you know what? She had an abortion, and William drove her to the doctor's to get it. They came over for coffee one morning and told me they did it as an assertion of a woman's rights over her own body, a 'symbolic gesture.' That's what they called it, a 'symbolic gesture.' They didn't even tell me she was pregnant until after the abortion. They didn't even tell me. You're a grandmother at least." She turned to the cookie jar and jerked the lid off. "Now, do you want a goddamned Oreo or not?" she said.

Janet turned and made her way through the kitchen. "No, no cookies," she said.

Barbara slammed the lid back on, and broke it in two. She let out a high-pitched cry, then calmly, quietly said, "That was one of our original wedding presents. That was one of our original wedding presents." She stood holding two pieces of teddy bear head in her hands, then threw them in the sink. "What about your husband?" she went on. She followed Janet back to the table. "What about George? You've got such a terrible family, a rotten life, he probably doesn't sleep with you anymore, right? Am I right?" She sat directly across from Janet and put her palms flat on the table. "Am I right?"

"We don't sleep together as often as I'd like, if that's what you mean," Janet said.

"Hell, that's not what I mean," Barbara said. "I've got such a perfect family, a perfect life? Sure. Jack hasn't slept with me in five months. In five whole months he hasn't so much as put a cold hand on my chest."

Janet stood up and started for the door. "I think I better be going," she said.

"Going, hell. You haven't heard the half of it yet." Barbara followed Janet to the door, even helped her open it. "He hasn't slept with me in five months, and do you know why?" she said. "He's been mowing the lawn. He's been mowing our lawn. For the past five months, every time I want to make love he says the lawn needs mowing, and he goes out to the garage, starts the mower, and goes to it." They were already down the steps and out on the lawn, Janet walking very slowly, Barbara right behind her. "I thought he was bored with me, so last week I went out and bought a Lipstick Red merry widow. One hundred and five dollars. That night I put it on and told him I wanted to make passionate love. You know what he did?" Barbara heard her voice outside. It sounded strangely muffled, almost quiet. She spoke louder. "He went right down to the garage and started the mower and cut the grass, then he got out the weed-eater and trimmed all the hedges, and then he got out the hand-clippers and trimmed the entire yard on his hands and knees. I watched for three hours from our bedroom window, Jack down there on the grass with the clippers in one hand, a flashlight in the other. We've got the best-manicured lawn in the whole tract. How's that for your perfect family?"

They were at the car now. Janet fumbled with the door handle, opened it and climbed in. Barbara pulled the keys from her robe pocket and gave them to Janet. "Here's your keys," she said.

"Thanks," Janet said. "Thanks a lot." She tried several keys in the ignition before she found the right one. "Thanks a whole lot," she said, and started backing the car off the lawn.

Barbara walked alongside as it slowly backed out. "And what about my lawn? What about my lawn? You have any idea how long it's going to take Jack to fix this lawn? He'll be out here every night for a month just trying to make it look like it used to. The police are coming. They're on their way right now and I'm telling them exactly where you live and they're going to come over and haul you away. Hah. That'll be a good one."

Janet put the car in forward and started moving on down the street. She smiled and waved at Barbara, who jogged alongside. "They'll come and haul you away, and then you'll be sorry you ever even came over here," Barbara said. She stopped running, and the car pulled away. Janet waved over her shoulder.

Barbara stood in the middle of the street, and pulled the robe closed on her chest. She looked up and down the street, but saw no one, then went up the steps and into the house.

She sat at the table and sipped her now tepid coffee, then went to the kitchen and brought from the cabinet under the sink a claw hammer. She calmly chased the teddy bear pieces around the inside of the sink with the hammer, smashing the broken head to dust. She tried to remember how bidding opened in pinochle.

Burglars

We stood in front of the Springers' house, Gary Erickson with his .410, Henry Forrester with a Luger, and me with a 30.06. We were pointing our guns at two burglars holding Ted and Mary Springer's television set, ready to load it into the back of their van.

It was midafternoon. Ted and Mary were on vacation out at Lake Havasu. The burglars, who looked like teenagers, apparently thought they could pull up in the driveway, break in, and walk out with whatever they could lay their hands on. They hadn't counted on good neighbors.

Margie had been at the sink getting a glass of water. I was watching a ball game. She called out, "Larry, the Springers know anyone with a van?"

I needed another beer, and so I got up and went to the kitchen. "Hell, I don't know," I said. I looked out the window. About this time two boys with half-grown beards and filthy T shirts came out the front door carrying a stereo.

"Holy shit," I said. I said, "Margie, get hold of the police. Those are burglars."

Gary and Henry had come out of their houses about the same

time I had, Henry from next door on the Springers' other side, Gary from across the street. Gary stood at the foot of the Springers' driveway, Henry directly across from me on the opposite edge of the Springers' yard.

I didn't know what to do. I only knew I wasn't going to take a shot at these guys, not if I could help it. And I knew Margie was on the phone to the police.

"Gary," I said. "Gary, what do you think?"

This was the first time I had spoken to him in seven months. We had had a falling-out. This was no time to keep up the fight, and I wanted to know what he thought of the situation. He was something of a hothead, a real go-getter. He wasn't far off from being a Direct Distributor for Amway, which, if you know anything at all about that operation, is pretty high up.

But Gary didn't answer me. He only opened the hand he held around the barrel of his gun and then regripped.

I looked over at Henry, who stood with his arm out stiff, pointing the Luger at the burglars. He was wearing a tank T shirt and gray work pants, and he was sweating. Henry was German, an older fellow, and had served in the German Army during World War II. He looked like some kind of marksmanship poster, feet evenly spread, arm out, body perpendicular to the direction he pointed the gun.

"Hey, Henry," I called. "Hey, what do you think?" But he didn't answer, either. I hadn't expected him to. I hadn't spoken to him in a good year or so.

It had been Amway, in fact, over which Gary and I had our falling-out. Gary and Nancy, his wife, had been our best friends, playing four-handed poker with us every Wednesday night for years. We always played at their house and used to stay up till all hours, filling the house with cigarette smoke and drinking margaritas, all the time listening to Tijuana Brass or the Beatles. Afterward I would carry my oldest daughter Melanie, Margie carrying Stephanie, back home across dew-wet grass, both girls asleep.

We'd carried on our Wednesday night card tradition until about a year ago.

Gary and Nancy had Amway meetings to go to twice a month, always on Wednesday nights. As soon as we started playing cards again, Gary started in on us about the world of Amway, about how it's the American way, and how you could make a swell income out of the thing if you had enough initiative, or you could just supplement your income with it. "Or you could be a clown and work your way through life," Gary would end up saying, "always putting out for someone else, always breaking your back so someone else can make a buck."

"But Gary," I would say to him, "I'm already a salesman. You don't think I have enough worries getting buyers to place end caps and island displays of soda pop every day? You think I want to sell more? Peddle soap?"

This was where he sprang the secret of Amway: it wasn't the selling of a product, but an investment in the future. By this time I would signal Margie, and we'd go back in their den, wake up Mel and Steffi, and make them walk home behind us in the wet grass. I wasn't a dummy. The secret of Amway wasn't selling a product, but talking people into working for you. I did enough conning every time I had to sell a display, every time I had to lie about a case cost discount, or try to sneak an extra hundred cases in to supermarket back rooms. We stopped our Wednesday night poker games.

Then one night about seven months ago we got an invitation from Gary and Nancy for dinner at their house, on a Wednesday night.

Because it was the polite thing to do, we went to an Amway meeting after dinner. We were driven there in the Ericksons' leased Mercedes. On the way over we were told about Gary's going full-time with Amway, and about the tax write-offs, and about the company trips to Hawaii and Vegas.

The meeting, held in an industrial park warehouse in Anaheim, turned out to be a mass orientation meeting for new Amway people, and those not quite ready to make the leap. We took our seats, and a man in an expensive-looking three-piece suit walked up on the stage. He gave a speech about how he had started out as a butcher working at a Ralph's in Lynwood, and how it had taken him only three years to go from a beat-up Pinto to a brand-new Porsche, and not just one Porsche, but two—his and hers. A woman got up and told pretty much the same story, and then another person got up, and then another, until the crowd was cheering over how much money could be made, how many cars could be bought, and how little time it could take.

We saw an Amway promotional film. Smiling girls at the Amway plant packaged soap and shampoo, while the narrator told of the original founding fathers who discovered the recipe for a kind of miracle soap by mixing a bunch of stuff together in a bathtub. An American flag snapping in the wind was shown several times during the film.

I'm a salesman from way back, and I knew that all those American flags and that talk of money and cars and security were just gimmicks to get you in on the bottom level. I have to admit that some of what was going on—especially the bits about the flag and the beautiful girls smiling—started to make my mouth water for the money.

But I held off. I knew that for every person who came up and talked about how much money he or she made in how little time, there were probably a thousand Amway reps at home, laundry rooms filled to the ceiling with various Amway products, and no place to sell the stuff. Fiscally speaking, more people died from Amway than made it to the stage by a long shot. It was a reflection on how weak people were. I knew all about weakness. I was a salesman. I preyed upon people's weaknesses, consumers and store managers alike. Who in his right mind would pour chemicals and carbonated water down his throat? Millions of Americans did every day. That is how I made my living.

After the meeting we went into a smaller room in the complex. Hors d'oeuvres, pastries, coffee and tea and milk had all been laid out, and the socializing began. Gary started introducing me around, Nancy taking Margie aside and doing the same. I met about fifty people, and I cannot remember a single name now. But I do remember their cars, which is how Gary introduced people to me. He would say, "Larry, I want you to meet ———. He has a DeLorean," or, "Larry, this is ———. Bought a brand-new Fiat convertible for his daughter last week."

While making the rounds, I happened to see across the room a woman I recognized from somewhere. She was beautiful, with dark hair to her shoulders, and an off-the-shoulder dress that showed the beginnings of her smooth back. She glanced over at me, then started working her way through the crowd toward us.

Her name was Elise, I remembered, but I could not recall her last name. I hadn't seen her in about fifteen years. It was quite a coincidence. She smiled, and her teeth were still as white and perfect as I remembered. We had dated a few times right out of high school, when I was a freshman in college trying to dodge the draft. We worked together at a restaurant in Costa Mesa. She was a waitress there, I was a cook. This was all years before Margie came around.

She came up to me and gave me a hug that nearly killed me. She pushed her breasts up against me, and started wiggling around and laughing. She kissed me, and I felt her tongue dart across my lips. I looked over her shoulder, and there was Gary, grinning, shaking his head, and looking at me. He gave me the okay sign with his fingers.

"I take it you've met?" he said. Elise pulled away.

She said, "Gary, why didn't you tell me you knew my old boyfriend Larry? Why didn't you tell me, you creep?" She went over to Gary and kissed him, too.

Turned out she was divorced, and for obvious reasons I started entertaining thoughts I shouldn't have had. I wanted to say something to her, but she smiled and went back into the crowd. She stopped and kissed another man.

After the meeting the four of us were walking out in the parking lot, heading for Gary's car. Nancy and Margie were behind us, talking about something to do with Amway jewelry.

Gary said, very quietly, "So, I see you've also been introduced to some of the other benefits of the American way."

"What do you mean by that?"

"You can't believe some of the tail I've nabbed around here, Larry," he whispered, then laughed. "I saw you and Elise. You've got the jump on a lot of other guys, let me tell you." He put his arm on my shoulder.

This, I knew, was the final pitch. I also knew that what he was proposing as being an Amway benefit was nowhere in their manifesto. He was just trying to get me in under him any way he could. Money, cars, girls.

Which is why I turned around then and hit him in the jaw. But either I hadn't landed my fist in the right spot or he had a jaw made of brick. He didn't flinch, and my hand felt as if it were broken.

He threw a fist in my gut, and I doubled over. Then he pushed me over with one hand, and I lay there in the parking lot. Margie and Nancy screamed.

I looked up at Gary. "You're a loser," he said. He turned and headed for his car, half-dragging Nancy. Margie knelt over me.

Now, our three guns pointed at the burglars, I didn't have an idea in hell what Gary was going to do.

I couldn't tell what Henry would do, either. Not that we were enemies. He was a widower, a little dumpy, but you could tell by looking at him that he'd been good-looking at one time. He had a fine jawline and thick salt-and-pepper hair. I probably knew him better than anyone else on the block, which was why I couldn't tell how he'd react in this situation.

Henry owned and operated a German delicatessen in Fountain Valley near the Sav-On on Magnolia. For years I would drop by there on my way home from work to pick up some of his kielbasa, which he made by hand. He let me come into the back of the shop one evening and watch him pump the inside stuff into the gut, the red spicy meat shooting through the casing in short, quick spurts he controlled with a foot pedal. He'd squeeze off a shot, twist the casing, then give it another shot, and on and on until he had twenty feet of kielbasa lengths. Before I left the store, he was always sure to give me a little something for the girls, like an extra pickle or, at Christmastime, some butter cookies.

That is, up until about a year and a half ago. One night Margie woke me up, shouting, "There's a fire, there's a fire!" I opened my eyes. The far wall in our bedroom was all orange and red, but it was not on fire.

I went to the bedroom window. A house on the block behind us and a few doors down was in flames. The fire had shown through our window onto the wall. I went into the girls' room to make sure they were all right, and found them sitting on their beds, looking out the window at the fire. It was no use telling them to go back to bed.

I was worried the fire might jump around, some sparks possibly landing on our roof and taking the whole house along with it, and so I went outside into the garage, got out the ladder, and turned the garden hose on. I climbed up on the roof and started spraying down the shake shingles, soaking them down good so that anything landing there wouldn't go up.

My view of the fire was spectacular. There was a built-in pool in the backyard of the burning house, and I could see the orange reflection of the flames on the water. The fire trucks were down there, and firemen were spraying everything down, the high arcs of water silhouetted by the flames.

I looked down the row of houses on our street, and saw Henry standing on his cinderblock back wall two houses away. He was watching the fire in his pajamas, his hands down at his sides.

"Henry," I called to him, but he didn't move. I figured he couldn't hear me for the fire engines.

I came down off the roof and then climbed onto our back wall.

I started walking along the wall to Henry's house, my arms out on either side to keep my balance. I walked along the Springers' back wall, and saw no lights on in their place. I guess they slept through the whole thing. Then I came up next to Henry. He still hadn't noticed me.

I said, "It's terrible."

He said nothing. I looked at him closer. His mouth hung open, and his face was covered with sweat.

"Henry," I said. "Henry, you all right?"

He only muttered something in German.

We stood like that for a few minutes, the two of us balanced up on his brick fence, staring at the fire. I glanced over at him from time to time. Each time I looked at him his face was sweatier and sweatier, and it seemed his mouth was open wider. He kept mumbling louder and louder until, by the time the heat started getting to me and the smoke had started smarting my eyes, he was speaking German in a normal voice, as though he were addressing the fire. One of the words he said over and over again sounded like the name Angelica.

I looked at him again, and the fire shone in his face until it was almost as orange as the flame itself. The colors moved across his face, making the folds of flesh around his jaw and neck look as if the skin rolled back and forth.

Then came a loud *pop*. I turned back to the burning house. The windows were bursting now, glass shooting out into the yard and pool. The glass skittering across the orange water made me think of Henry's face, and I looked back at him.

He was shaking. I knew the old man was going to fall over, and then the sliding glass door off the patio and pool burst. The sound was like that of a bomb exploding.

Henry tottered forward. I grabbed his shirt and pulled him back, but pulled him too far. We fell back into a row of oleander bushes growing along his back wall. The thick hedge cushioned our fall, Henry landing more on me than the ground. I got the wind knocked out of me and lay there on the grass, my knees up, my arms out to either side. I looked straight up into the night, and saw sparks flying around, high up in the smoke and ash and steam. In that moment when it seemed I would never breathe again, I thought: I am going to die, here and now, and one of those sparks will land on my roof and devour my wife, my two daughters, and my home.

When I got my breath back, Henry helped me up and into his house. We went through the kitchen into the living room, where he sat me down on the couch. He fell back into an easy chair across from me.

I looked around the room and noticed there was no television set. He had a row of bookcases along one wall, his easy chair, the sofa I sat on, a coffee table, and an end table centered against the far wall, across from the bookcases. On the end table was a framed black-and-white photograph, wallet-size and faded to brown. About a dozen paintings and photographs of cathedrals, those big old drafty things you see on postcards from Europe, decorated the walls.

I looked back at Henry. He was leaning forward in his chair, his hands clasped between his knees, his head down.

I took a deep breath. I felt like I'd bruised a couple of ribs. I put my hand on my side and said, "Are you okay?"

Without looking up from the floor, he said, "I saw bombs fall. I saw my home burn. I saw my wife die."

He gave out a breath that seemed to empty him. He was silent. Then he whispered, "Angelica, Angelica."

I struggled up from the couch, my hand still pressed on my side, and went over to the end table. I looked at the photo.

It was a picture of Henry and, I imagine, Angelica. Henry stood at a three-quarter angle to the camera. He was grinning, the same grin he gave when slipping a few free cookies into my bag at the delicatessen. He wore a gray suit with a thin black tie and white shirt. His hands were behind him, his thick black hair slicked back. He hadn't looked into the camera lens when the shot had been taken.

Angelica wore a light-colored dress. She was fair-skinned, with dark, dark eyes and black hair. Unlike Henry, she had looked into the lens, and was smiling. She was holding a bouquet of flowers.

I went over to Henry. I wanted to put my hand on his shoulder and say something to make him feel better, anything, but I heard him whispering words that sounded like "*Dermorders, Dermorders,*" and I decided not to touch him. Instead I left, closing the front door behind me, and then I looked in the window. He had started rocking back and forth very slowly, his lips moving. He hadn't seen me leave.

Next morning I looked out the bedroom window. The house had burned down to the ground. The water in the pool was black, a layer of burnt wood and ash floating in it. We saw less and less of Henry. Eventually he gave the shop over to a submarine sandwich chain.

But here was Henry pointing a Luger at the burglars. I could imagine him drawing a bead, muttering, "Murderers, murderers," and then emptying the gun on them.

A drop of sweat rolled into my eye. I took a hand down from my gun and rubbed my eyes. I wondered when the police would come.

It was then that the bigger of the two burglars leaned his head back and let out a deep, rolling laugh. His hair was pulled back in a ponytail. The ponytail quivered as he laughed.

He said, "You bunch of assholes. You go ahead and shoot us. See what happens. Go ahead."

He smiled, showing he had several teeth missing. He gave his partner a shove with the set. They started moving toward the van.

I glanced over at Henry, who seemed to point his arm and the gun even straighter, stiffer. I saw Gary cock back the hammer on his shotgun.

But of course it was me who fired. I pulled the trigger, and put a hole dead center in the TV tube. The tube exploded, the burglars dropped the television. The set hit the ground at an awkward angle, rolled onto its back, and lay there.

The burglars didn't move. I looked over at Henry and Gary. Gary had brought his gun down, as had Henry, whose arm hung limp at his side. They were both watching me. They looked as if they were waiting for something.

Night

He woke up. He thought he could hear their child's breathing in the next room, the near-silent, smooth sound of air in and out.

He touched his wife. The room was too dark to let him see her, but he felt her movement, the shift of blanket and sheet.

"Listen," he whispered.

"Yesterday," she mumbled. "Why not yesterday," and she moved back into sleep.

He listened harder; though he could hear his wife's breath, thick and heavy next to him, there was beneath this the thin frost of his child's breathing.

The hardwood floor was cold beneath his feet. He held out a hand in front of him, and when he touched the doorjamb, he paused, listened again, heard the life in his child.

His fingertips led him along the hall and to the next room. Then he was in the doorway of a room as dark, as hollow as his own. He cut on the light.

The room, of course, was empty. They had left the bed just as their child had made it, the spread merely thrown over bunched and wrinkled sheets, the pillow crooked at the head. The small blue desk was littered with colored pencils and scraps of construction paper, a bottle of white glue.

He turned off the light and listened. He heard nothing, then backed out of the room and moved down the hall, back to his room, his hands at his sides, his fingertips helpless.

This happened each night, like a dream, but not.

Garage Sale

"How much for this?" the woman from across the street said. She was holding up a turquoise-and-milk-colored candy dish, something we'd gotten as a wedding present and had never used. The box it came in still had pieces of tape on it, corners of silver paper here and there.

People were milling around on our driveway, picking through what we had for sale on the old folding tables Liz had borrowed from school. Lisa and Adrienne were out on the street, riding bikes in endless figure eights. For a moment I thought to tell them to get out of the street, but decided not to. They were old enough. They knew what to do if they saw any cars.

Then I looked for Liz, saw her standing in the carport talking with a woman I didn't recognize from anywhere. The woman pulled out a wallet from the purse she held, handed some bills to Liz. Liz smiled without looking at the cash, and folded it in half, put it in her jeans pocket. I didn't even know what she'd sold.

I turned back to the lady from across the street. She still held the candy dish and was looking at me, waiting.

I shrugged, put a hand to my neck. The dish was ugly, I knew that much. "I don't know," I said. "A dollar?"

She smiled, the same sort of smile she'd given each time I'd named a price so far: a dollar for the spice rack, fifty cents for the mayonnaise server, five dollars for the electric rotisserie, all of it stuff we'd never used. Her smile was one that didn't show any teeth, only the corners of her mouth turned up. Prim was the word that came to me first, then the word Cheap.

She handed me the dollar, put the candy dish and mayonnaise server in the rotisserie pan, set the rotisserie on the spice rack box; she hadn't collected things as she went, only asked prices and handed me money. She picked the stack of things up, turned from the table.

She said, "You two ought to get together to get your prices straight, you and your wife. I don't want you to think I'm cheating you or anything. But ten minutes ago I asked your wife how much the candy dish was, and she told me five dollars. She told me fifteen for the rotisserie." She still had the same smile. "I'm telling you this just so you'll know. For future reference." She walked to the foot of the driveway, looked both ways, and crossed the street. My daughters, still making figure eights, only drove around her. They didn't even look at her, and for some reason I was glad for that.

The plan was to sell off as much junk as possible in order to save some of the moving allowance Liz had been given. Then when we got up to Tempe, where Liz would be an assistant principal in a new school district opening up, we wouldn't have the dead weight of unused wedding gifts, no accumulated junk of nine years of marriage and two kids.

Late last night we'd gone to Sandburg and hauled three folding tables down dark linoleum halls. The girls skipped, laughed, called out each other's names to hear their echoes, while Liz and I carried one table at a time, loaded each into the back of the station wagon. We drove home slowly, streets empty, tables bouncing and creaking behind us, and this morning we'd gotten up at seven, started laying things out. People were going through the junk before we'd even finished filling up the tables.

Now it was near ten, and there was still plenty of stuff lined up against the carport wall, everything from three Formica cutting boards and a hibachi to two Big Wheels and a playpen.

I put the money the woman had given me in my pants pocket, along with the rest I'd collected so far, what I figured was somewhere around forty dollars, then went past the tables and people to Liz, still in the carport.

She was bent over one of the boxes there, and I watched as she pulled out a copper kettle, an old Thermos, a wooden salad bowl, each item wrapped in newspaper. I couldn't remember seeing any of it before.

She stood, the kettle in her hand. "From Scott and Maureen," she said. She didn't look at me, but held the kettle to her face, breathed on it, rubbed the spot with her palm. "Ten dollars?" she said. She smiled.

"Don't ask me," I said. I bent over, picked up the Thermos. It looked familiar now, blue with gray diamonds around it. I said, "How much have you made so far?"

"Counting your recliner?"

I figured she was joking, gave a small laugh. I said, "Very funny."

She pulled the bills out of her jeans pocket, folded out four tens and three twenties. "One hundred dollars," she said, the bills flat in her hand. She was looking at me now. "It's no joke. She asked me if I had any furniture for sale and I brought her into the house for a minute. Mrs. White is her name. She offered the money. I took it."

She nodded to something behind me, and I turned, saw the old woman Liz had talked to a few moments before. She held up a pine napkin holder, looked at it, put it down. Liz said, "And a hundred dollars is just for the recliner. I imagine around sixty or so for the odds and ends I've sold so far."

I turned to her, could feel my teeth together too tight, my face going hot. "What the hell's the idea here?"

"The idea," she said, quiet and cool, "is what we already agreed upon. We agreed to get out of this place. You started it. I'm just following through." She put the bills back in her pocket, bent to the box again. This time she pulled out a black metal desk lamp, no bulb. "She's coming back tonight," she said, "to look the rest of our furniture over. She might buy everything in the house. If we're lucky." She handed me the lamp. "Here," she said. "Five dollars."

She was right. I'd been the one who'd wanted us away from here. But I think I had good reason.

A month ago I got a call to sub at Sandburg, and after a morning of baby-sitting junior high kids in social studies all I'd wanted was to sit down and have lunch with my wife. I went into the cafeteria, through the line to pick up my beefaroni and pear with cottage cheese, and saw the faculty tables at the opposite end of the room. I weaved between tables of screaming preteens and finally made it to where Liz sat, her lunch already half-eaten. I sat down opposite her, but before I could settle in, unfold my napkin, or even say hello to Liz, a man sat down next to her.

He was thin with a mustache and pointed beard, and he didn't even look at me, though Liz's eyes were right on mine. She didn't blink as the man reached across her tray for her milk carton, picked it up and took a sip, smiling at her all this time. He put the carton back down. Liz's hands were on the tabletop, holding tight the edges of her tray.

"Hey," the man said, and with two fingers he reached up to Liz's hair, lifted a strand and gently tucked it behind her ear. He still hadn't looked at me. Liz still hadn't looked away from me.

"Michael," she said, and the man leaned closer to her, still smiling. She said, "This is my husband, Greg."

The man turned quickly, blinked twice, but just kept smiling. Then he put out his hand for me to shake. There was nothing I could do, of course, but take it, and feel on the man's fingertips the cold wet of condensation from my wife's milk carton.

That evening, after the girls were in bed, we were in the living room watching CNN, no lights on in the house. When the second round of the same news started up, I said, "You have kids, you know."

How far the Dow Jones had slipped that day came on again. The numbers were still the same.

She said, "What are you talking about?"

"You have a husband, too."

She turned to me, the only color to her the shattered light from the TV screen, the commercials there. She said, "Are these supposed to be things I don't know?"

We said nothing else until after we'd gone to bed. The house was so quiet I thought I could hear the girls breathing in the next room. I was on my back, my hands behind my head. Liz was turned from me and on her side, facing the wall.

That was when I started it. I said, "Let's just move from here. Let's get out of here."

A few moments passed, and I thought I could still hear their breathing. Then Liz said, "How far?"

"You name it," I said.

She rolled over, faced me. She propped herself on an elbow. She said, "Phoenix. Flagstaff, maybe." She paused. "Denver."

I rolled over, my back to her.

Two weeks later she'd gotten the interview in Tempe; a week later she'd been offered the assistant principal job. A week after that we'd struggled with folding tables down the dark hall of a junior high so that today we could have the garage sale.

At six-thirty the doorbell rang, and Liz got up from the table, wiped her mouth with one of the thin napkins that came with the bucket of chicken. A few bones were heaped on a community paper plate at the center of the table, half-empty containers of cole slaw and mashed potatoes next to it. Lisa and I'd bought the chicken while Liz and Adrienne straightened up after the sale. We'd made two hundred and six dollars.

"She told me she wouldn't be over until seven," Liz said, and tossed the napkin on the table.

"Who, Mommy?" Adrienne asked, and then Lisa said, "Who?"

I said, "Don't talk with your mouth full."

Liz smiled back at them as she neared the door. She said, "Mrs. White," and then opened the door.

It was the woman from across the street.

"Oh," Liz said, one hand on the knob, the other on her hip. "Hi. What can I do for you?"

"It's about the rotisserie," she said. "Your husband sold it to me?" Her hands were in front of her, then with one of them she reached up, touched her blue-gray hair just above her ear.

Liz looked at me, then back to the woman. "Yes?"

"Well," she said, and brought her hands together again. "It seems there's a piece missing. A drip tray that slides in beneath the pan?" She was looking at me now, and I thought I could see on her face that same smile. Liz turned to me then, too.

I put a drumstick on the community plate. "I wouldn't know anything about that," I said, and took a sip at my beer.

The woman said, "I suppose it's just a rectangular tray. Frank and I have already started with this roast, and it's dripping down through the pan and onto the counter. Are you sure—"

"Listen," I said, and as soon as the word left me I knew it was too loud. I could feel my daughters' eyes on me now, thought I saw Liz move a little, the woman back up an inch or so.

I said, "Listen," again, and I let it come out of me just as loud. I stood, wiped my hands with one of the napkins. "We just sold the thing to you, and how we sold it to you is how we got it." I paused. "That's for future reference. Just so you'll know." I was moving through the living room now, my steps maybe too slow. I was at the recliner now, the one already sold, and I dropped the wadded napkin on the seat, moved toward them at the door.

Liz said, "Greg?" and the woman backed up a few more inches, but then she stopped. Liz was looking at me, her mouth open.

The woman said, "Now we bought this rotisserie in good faith. Good faith that all the parts were there. Now I think I'll have to ask for my money back."

I was almost at the door. Liz hadn't moved, still watched me, but I only looked at the woman, stared at her until her eyes fell from mine. I said, "Sorry."

"Well then," she said, and I could see her fingers just touching, trembling. "Well," she said. Her eyes wouldn't come back to mine. "I think that I'll just have to go see my husband about this. I'm going to have to speak to Frank about this."

I said, "Send him on over. We can talk about it."

She backed up a few more inches, then turned, headed off the porch and onto the driveway, where three empty folding tables still stood.

Liz slammed the door closed. She said, "Now just what the hell was that all about?" Her hands were on her hips, her face only inches from mine.

"Mommy?" Adrienne said, and we both turned to the kids. They sat with their hands in their laps, watching. "Mommy?" Adrienne said again, and I could see her bottom lip giving way.

"Just a minute," Liz said, smiling at them. She turned to me, whispered, "Come with me." She headed down the hall behind her, back to the bedroom.

"Just a minute," I said to my daughters, and I tried my best to give them some smile they might believe. "Finish dinner," I said.

Liz was sitting on the bed. She was looking in the dresser mirror, just staring. "What the hell is wrong with you?" she said, but on her words I couldn't hear any anger. Only her voice, flat and dead.

"Me?" I said. "What about you?" I sat on the edge of the bed a few feet away from her. "You're the one selling off the furniture."

She said, "You're the one who told us to get out of here, to start over. And I'm the one making things go." She paused a moment, her voice still the same dead tone. "Can't you see I want to go?"

She stood up, went to the dresser. She put both hands to the edge, leaned her weight against it. She was still looking into the mirror, her face straight on. From where I sat I could see two of her, a profile staring into a profile, her eyes tired, her mouth closed.

I looked away from her, rubbed my hands back and forth on my thighs.

"Mommy?" I heard. This time it was Lisa.

"Just a minute!" I called out, trying to make my voice true. I rubbed my hands on my thighs again. I took in a breath, held it. I opened my mouth to speak.

But nothing came. Instead, I stopped moving my hands and slowly held out one of them, the left. I held it in front of me, straight and flat.

My hand was shaking. I wasn't sure if it was only blood through me or the fight I knew was coming. The fight I'd known was coming from the moment the man had touched her hair, put her straw to his lips.

I looked up at Liz. She stared into the mirror a moment longer, then closed her eyes, let her head drop. She was still leaning on her hands, and for an instant I thought I could see a gray patch of condensation on the mirror.

Then it disappeared, and she turned around.

She said, "So what do you want to know? Do you want to know places? Dates? Do you want to know how many times? Do you want to know what he thinks of my moving? What?"

But I looked back at my hand, then placed the other one next to it, both hands there in the air, trembling.

I said, "Nothing. I don't want to know anything," and I knew it was the truth.

The doorbell rang then, and I stood, not wanting to see her eyes, not wanting hers to find me. "That's probably Frank," I said, and moved past her, opened the door and went down the hall.

My knees felt thin as I reached the door. My knees felt like paper.

I glanced back at the girls, who still sat with their hands in their laps, uneaten food before them. Lisa said, "Daddy, what's wrong?" Adrienne looked at her sister, then back at me.

"Just hold on a minute," I said. I didn't even try to smile for them this time, and I pulled open the door.

There stood an older woman, her purse held at her chest with both hands. I looked at her a moment, then recognized the white hair, the blue-flowered dress, the thick stockings. This was the woman who'd bought my recliner.

I stepped back, my knees even thinner now.

Then Liz's hand was at the small of my back, and I felt it linger there as she came from behind me and to the door.

"Mrs. White," she said, and put out a hand to the woman.

"I'm sorry I'm so early," she said. She stepped into the house.

Liz said, "Mrs. White, this is my husband, Greg."

I still hadn't spoken, hadn't moved. The woman held out her hand to me. She said, "Nice to meet you."

"I'm sorry," I finally said. I shook her hand. "I'm just—" I started, and I took a breath. "I just thought it was somebody else at the door," I said. But I wasn't thinking about Frank or about this woman about to try to buy all our furniture. I was thinking about my wife's hand still at the small of my back, and about the feeling in my knees, the condensation of her breath on the mirror.

Then Liz's hand was gone, and she was leading Mrs. White into our living room. "These are our children," Liz said. "Lisa Marie and Adrienne Anne."

"Hi," they said together, and they began to eat again.

I started to close the door, but stopped, looked at the house across the street. I saw no one.

"I find this a little strange," Mrs. White said, and I turned to her. She stood next to the recliner, one hand on it, gently rubbing it. She looked at Liz, then me, then the sofa before her. "I'm not in the habit of this," she said, smiling. "But I have a niece who's getting married, and they don't have any money whatsoever, so I figure this is what a great-aunt is for, for helping out." She paused a moment, put both hands to her purse again. She glanced up at the ceiling. "So when you told me this morning that not only was this recliner for sale, but everything else, I took that to mean some sign for me to do what I could. A sign for me to do the right thing." She laughed a moment, her shoulders moving up and down. "I know that sounds strange, my thinking it's a sign. But I'm an old woman." She laughed again.

"Makes perfect sense to me," Liz said, and glanced at me, smiling. I couldn't tell what she meant by smiling at me, whether it was an act for this woman, or if there was something more. I wondered what would make perfect sense for us here, now.

"So where to begin?" Mrs. White said. She straightened her shoulders, lost the smile. She was looking at Liz.

Liz said, "Why not the sofa?"

Mrs. White moved to it, ran her hand across the arm, the material—navy blue corduroy—still in good shape despite two children and the fact we'd bought it a month after we were married. Mrs. White patted one of the cushions, sat on it. Then she stood, the purse in her hands again. She looked at the sofa, tilted her head. The girls were still eating, and I could see Lisa's legs beneath the table, swinging away.

"One fifty," the woman said.

I moved from the door then, put a hand to the sofa, ran it across the arm just as she had. I crossed my arms, stepped back from it, looked at it.

I turned to Mrs. White, said, "One hundred."

She seemed frightened somehow, her eyebrows drawn up, her mouth closed tight.

Liz said, "You mean two hundred. Two hundred, right?"

I looked at her. "No," I said. "One hundred. One hundred

dollars seems about right to me." I paused. "One hundred dollars makes perfect sense to me."

The woman held her purse even more tightly now. She looked at the two of us again. A smile, quick and broken, came to her face. She said, "I'm willing to pay that. One hundred." She paused, her eyes on the sofa again. "One hundred. If that's fair."

"It's fair," I said.

"Greg," Liz said, but I had already turned to the loveseat, slapped my hand on one of the cushions.

"Fifty," I said, and I was smiling now. Liz stood behind the woman, whose purse seemed to inch up her chest the tighter she held it.

"Greg," Liz said again.

I said, "Liz."

She brought a hand to her forehead, the move too quick, I could see, but then she let it slip to her cheek, held her fingers there against the soft skin I'd thought I knew better than my own.

Her face was blank a moment, then something came back into her, her cheeks suddenly alive, her eyes open wide.

"Forty," she said. "Forty dollars." She was looking at me, and I wondered what she saw. If it was only her husband next to a blue corduroy loveseat, I decided, that was enough. That was plenty.

"Forty sounds good to me," I said, and Mrs. White turned to Liz, gave the same broken smile, then took a deep breath. She laughed again, her shoulders in the same movement up and down. She let go of the purse, let it hang by the strap so that it touched the carpet. She placed her free hand on her chest, took another deep breath.

"Forty it is, then," she said.

I said, "Now how about this lamp?" and went to the brass lampstand at the end of the loveseat, touched my fingers to the shade.

"Twenty?" Liz said.

"Fifteen," I said, and Lisa shouted from the table, "Ten!"

"Five!" Adrienne yelled, and I put up my hand to stop them all.

"Compromise," I said. "Compromise. This one is on the house. The lamp we'll throw in for free," and for a moment I tried to picture this woman's niece and husband-to-be, the truckload of furniture that would arrive soon wherever they lived, our old lives now new with them.

"Done and done," Liz said, and the girls laughed, Mrs. White smiling.

Liz went to the television then, put a hand up to it as though she were a game show hostess. She looked at me to give a price, but I nodded at her to start. I was thinking about Frank from across the street, trying to figure some way to help him out with the rotisserie. I could round up a small cookie sheet from the cupboard, give that to him. The fewer things we had to pack, the better.

Sleeping Through

The baby, in the crib at the foot of the bed, was sleeping through for the first time—he would be ten weeks on Thursday—and Paul and Kate lay awake in bed, listening. It was just past three, the usual time for the baby to wake up, for Paul to change the diaper, for Kate to lay the baby next to her in bed and nurse.

Paul lay on his back, his hands behind his head. He looked at the ceiling, trying to puzzle out in the darkness the shapes in the stipple up there. In daylight the shapes were rough sunflowers, but in the darkness they became only gray swirls, indistinguishable one from the next. He lay there and imagined the builder who had put up the stipple, imagined a man on a stepladder here in his bedroom, some sort of sunflower template in his hand, pressing it into the wet ceiling, pulling it back to reveal the shape with its circle of short leaves, its center of sharp brush strokes.

Then he imagined what the house must have been like when that worker had put up the ceiling. He saw the bedroom empty—no carpeting, just plywood planks. The walls were bare Sheetrock, spackle run in white lines up the walls and along the ceiling and baseboards. Downstairs the floor was cement, and in the kitchen there was no stove or refrigerator, no washer or dryer. No linoleum on the floor, the countertop only a wood frame, doorless cupboards, ceiling lights only wires hanging down.

Kate whispered, "Paul?"

"I'm here," he whispered.

"What are you thinking about?" She breathed, and he could feel her eyes on him as she lay next to him, the sheet and blanket pulled up to her chin.

He turned and looked at the clock. The pale green hands read three-thirty-three.

He whispered, "Nothing," and smiled to himself at the truth of this: his thoughts of an empty house. Nothing there.

"I'm scared," she said.

"Of what?"

"His sleeping through," she whispered. She turned onto her back.

He looked at her, saw she was staring at the ceiling just as he had been. He wondered if she could see in that ceiling what he had been able to see: first designs up there, then an entire house filled with nothing.

Finally Paul whispered, "Let's go down to the kitchen."

He pushed the sheets back, climbed out of bed all in a moment, as if they had gone to bed only minutes before and had never fallen asleep. Paul got to the doorway first and looked back.

Kate had stopped at the crib and was leaning over it. She was only a silhouette to him, a shape bent over the crib, and he thought that she could not possibly have seen the shapes in the ceiling, the ceiling man working there, the white plasterboard of the wall, the spackle even whiter. She was thinking of other things, he knew: the baby, his sleeping. And, he imagined, she was thinking of how her breasts might become engorged again and about the pain that would cause, the baby unable to nurse because the breast was too full, so that it would become a circle of pain for her: the baby crying for food, Kate holding too much food in her.

Then he heard the baby stir and for a moment felt relief, ready for the baby to awaken. Paul watched for Kate to lean even farther into the crib to pick him up. He listened for the small cry, the quick breaths in, but then she stood, moved from the crib.

He watched her coming toward him, and in the small brown light cast from the night-light in the hall she seemed a ghost to him, a gray nightgown floating across the room, a body with no face.

"He's not waking up," came her whispered voice, a voice he thought for an instant he could not recognize in the darkness.

He turned on each light in the kitchen: first the stove hood, then, from the switchplate across the kitchen, the small chandelier above the kitchen table and the ceiling fixture above the sink.

He turned from the switchplate, looked at her at the stove. Her nightgown wasn't gray, he saw, but a light violet, patterned with small purple flowers. Her nursing gown.

She had begun wearing it, he remembered, some two months before the baby had been born. The first time she had put it on, he had said, "Warming up?" and laughed.

He was already in bed. She stood at the dresser, and he watched as she leaned over to brush out her hair, her face turned to him. She smiled. "Sort of," she said. "I just want to feel what it's like. It's a comfortable nightgown regardless. So don't make fun."

He could see her breast through the opening in the nightgown, could see the white skin there, the pale pink nipple. He said, "I'm not," and when she had climbed into bed and turned out the light, he had slipped his hand into the gown, cupped his hand on her breast, and said, "All the easier to hold you with, my dear," and they had both laughed.

They made love that night, she above him, and when she sat up she pulled the gown off as if to reveal herself to him, and he placed his hands on the miraculous swelling before him, their baby already there. He moved his hands across her, then placed his mouth on her breast, drew the nipple out hard and taut, and wondered what her milk might taste like when it would finally come.

He looked at her now. Her face was blank, her hair everywhere. She pushed in a button for one of the burners, lifted the blue kettle from the stove. She brought it to the sink, turned the tap water on and filled it. For no good reason, more, he imagined, just to hear his voice, to make sure he was still alive, he said, "You scared me up there." He leaned against the counter, crossed his arms.

She rubbed her eyes as she carried the kettle to the stove. She said, "Why?"

"You looked like a ghost. In the dark you looked like the walking dead." He smiled.

She stopped, the kettle just above the burner, the coils now going red. She turned to him, slowly, as if she might still be asleep.

She said, "Don't talk like that."

He stopped smiling, put his hands at his sides, palms on the edge of the counter. "I was just talking," he said.

"But don't talk about that," she said. She still hadn't moved, still held the kettle above the burner.

"About what?" He put on a puzzled look for her, then went to the cupboard next to the stove, brought down two coffee mugs. He held them as if he had never felt their weight in his hands before.

She placed the kettle on the burner. She said, "Don't talk about death. About dying. Mine, yours. Anybody's. That's what."

He put the mugs on the counter. "You know I was just talking," he said. "You know I was just saying that. I wasn't talking about dying." He leaned against the counter again. He smiled again.

She turned from him and went to the kitchen table. She pulled out a chair, sat down. "Whatever," she said. She put her elbow on the table, her chin on her fist.

"What are you afraid of?" he said.

She didn't move. She said, "Plenty."

"Such as?"

She let out a breath, and he knew he should stop pushing her as he did. But he wanted to know.

He got the jar of instant coffee from the rack on the inside of the pantry door, then pulled a spoon from inside the silverware drawer. His back was to her as he carefully measured the coffee.

She said, "Like I already told you. Him, upstairs. I'm afraid of his sleeping through. I'm afraid he's not okay, that he's sick or something. That's one thing."

He turned around. The water was heating up now, the soft rumble of the kettle behind him. "He's sleeping," he said. "That's what we want, isn't it? For him to sleep through?" He said this but remembered the relief he had felt when, back in the bedroom, he had thought the baby was waking up. He felt that somehow, right now, he was lying to her.

"I know," she said. "I know we want him to sleep." She closed her eyes. "But can't you even let me have that? I can be afraid of that if I want, can't I?" She opened her eyes, leaned back in her chair. She let her hand drop to the table. She looked at him.

He shrugged. "If you want," he said. "But I don't see why you would."

From where he stood he could see the opening in her nursing gown, the white skin again. Above the skin he could see the edge of her nursing bra, this even whiter.

He went to the refrigerator, took out the carton of half-and-half.

"Now," she said to his back, "what are you afraid of?"

But he was already thinking about it. He was thinking about her, about how, a week ago, they had tried to make love for the first time since the baby was born, Kate having gone to the obstetrician two days before. The doctor had given her the okay.

He had tried to make something of the evening and had put a candle on the nightstand next to the bed, then brought the radio up from his workbench in the garage and set it next to the dresser. He tuned it to an easy-listening station and climbed into bed, waited for her to finish in the bathroom.

When she came out, she had on a white chemise, something from what seemed years ago. She got into bed, whispered, "We have to be quiet," and pointed to the crib.

"Fine," he whispered, and kissed her neck. She had on perfume.

They had gone slowly, and then, just before he entered her, she had held him close, whispered, "Go easy." He nodded, his eyes closed. Once inside her, though, he had opened his eyes, looked down at her.

Her face, shadowed by the candle, half in darkness, half in moving light, had been blank and pale. Then she flinched in pain, her legs moving up his back, her eyes squeezing shut, her lips pursed. At that moment he had closed his eyes and pulled away from her.

"Well?" she said.

He let the refrigerator door close, set the carton on the counter, all with his back to her. The water was boiling now, and he pushed the "off" button, filled the mugs. He opened the half-and-half and poured a small amount into each cup. Clouds rose from the bottom of the cups to the surface, changed the coffee from deep brown to tan.

He took the mugs to the table. He set one mug before her, then sat down.

She was looking at him. "Thanks for the coffee," she said, "but I'm still waiting." She picked up her coffee, touched it to her lips, winced.

He said, "Of you. I'm afraid of you." He looked down at his hands in his lap, then looked at the tablecloth, white vinyl with large red and blue and yellow tulips with long green stems. She had one hand on the tablecloth, and from where he sat it looked as if she were holding a bunch of flowers, her fingers curled over several stems.

He saw the hand turn palm up, the fingers go straight. She said, "Why?"

He shrugged. "Making love. That's what I'm afraid of. After the last time. What happened." He shrugged again, gave a small laugh. "Other than that, nothing," he said. He looked up at her.

She was looking at him, her eyes saddened, it seemed. She said, "No," and moved her hand toward him. "You can't be afraid of that. Not of making love."

He moved a hand to the table. A moment later they were holding hands, and he saw then what she was afraid of, saw, finally, what had happened an afternoon ten weeks before, Kate in the birthing chair, her feet in stirrups like the metal claws of some upturned dead animal, himself standing next to her, her pale wet hand in his.

The far wall of the delivery room had been one giant window, leaded squares of glass six inches thick mounted one on top of another like so many brittle bricks.The wall faced west, as did the birthing chair, and the room had been filled with light. He couldn't remember any lights having been on in the room. Just that wall, and the sun behind it.

The doctor, at the foot of the bed, there between her legs with his hands ready to catch, yelled, *Push*, and then Paul, too, had yelled, felt her squeeze down on his fingers, turning his own first red, then a light shade of blue. The nurses, one hovering just behind the doctor, the other holding his wife's other hand, urged her more gently. *Push, Kate,* they had whispered.

There it was. A baby, slick and a little blue, bluer than his fingers. The doctor brought it to the warming table across the room, the nurses wiping it clean. Then it had cried, this new, small voice in the room where before there had been nothing.

A boy, the doctor had said over his shoulder, his hands gently working the baby's now pink arms and legs, and Paul had realized then that they were now three. Three.

He looked at her now, before daylight in a kitchen with all its lights on, and felt for the first time the void he knew she had thought about before. He could look at a ceiling and imagine an empty house, but she could imagine it lifeless.

"Don't be afraid," she said, and moved her other hand toward him across the flowers of the tablecloth.

He looked at her. He swallowed, then blinked. He saw her come into focus, then waver out again. He rubbed his eyes with his free hand.

She held his hand with both hers now, held it even tighter. She said, "Paul," and the word meant many things to him at once.